Blue Rose

By
Darlene Chavis

Always Believe!
Darlene
Chavis

ISBN-13:978-1490942001
ISBN-10:1490942009

Dedicated to my loving husband Hurley.
Thank you for being my rock in the midst of the
storms, and for being my heart…always.

I Love You!

"Murphy! Dunbar! Your ride along is upstairs waiting for you. Get up there and remember, behave!"

"Yes, Sarge." We said in unison, in a mocking tone.

We hate ride alongs but we are always on our best behavior whenever we have one. Jack and I know how to have fun on patrol. But we also take our jobs very seriously. With our ride along this time, well let's just say we will definitely be watching our step for the next few nights.

"So are you ready for this one Murph?"

"You know how much I hate this Jack. But I guess it's something we have to do. Especially now with that new community outreach program the chief and the mayor want implemented."

"Well, let's go get him then."

When we get to the waiting area, the receptionist points to a man sitting across the room writing in a notebook. As we approach him, I notice that he looks rather young, younger than I expected actually. Not bad looking either. Maybe this won't be too awful after all.

"Ahem, ahem." Jack clears his throat so the young man will finally look up.

He jumps up out of his seat. Much taller than he looked from across the room, and actually much more handsome too. Short sandy color hair, green eyes, a chiseled face, he could've been a model. He has that sexy scruff on his face too, it doesn't look like he's bothered to shave for a few days. He has a rugged look to him for being a city boy.

He immediately extends his hand and shakes Jacks' and then mine. The moment our hands touch, I feel an instant shock, as if I have stuck a wet finger in an electrical socket. We pull our hands away instantly.

"Uh, hi, you must be my cops for the next few nights. I'm Benjamin Brewer, a reporter for the Philadelphia Sun."

"Hello, I'm Michele Murphy, and this is my partner Jack Dunbar. We just have some rules to go over with you, and you need to sign some papers, then we'll get rolling. Right this way."

We escort him back to the reception desk, and have him sign a release form and get him a flak jacket. We go over some rules, mainly telling him to stay in the car, don't get in our way, and never interfere with our job. Then we head for the squad car.

We have just climbed in the car and he starts with the questions right away.

"So, Michele, why would a girl like you want to be a police officer?" I shoot Jack a look and he smiles at me, he knows exactly what I am thinking. What the hell kind of a question is that?

"First of all Mr. Brewer, what do you mean by a *girl like me*?" This is not getting off to a good start.

"Oh, I didn't mean anything by that, but you're attractive and have a nice body. Why would you want to do a job like this?" Is this guy for real? What an ass!

"Let's get something straight right now Mr. Brewer. My looks have nothing to do with my choice of career. I enjoy my job, and I'm damn good at it, so I suggest you get any archaic, chauvinistic, stupid views you may have out of your little head for the next three nights, and we'll get along a lot better, okay? Furthermore, you will address me as Officer Murphy!"

Jack is snickering under his breath. The jerk in the back seat can't hear him, but I definitely can. He is trying his best to hold back from laughing.

"Well Officer Murphy, I'm sorry I offended you, I certainly didn't mean to. I was just trying to get some background information for my piece. It just seems to me that any woman, as pretty as yourself could have any job she chose, so why this one. That's all I was trying to ask. Plus, you are so, well, so tiny. How can you possibly be effective at your job?"

"Excuse me, I'll have you know that size means nothing. Well, at least not when it comes to being a police officer." I turn my head around so I can look him up and down with a smirk.

Jack jumps in at this point, I don't know if it's to save me or the reporter, but I am glad to get a reprieve from this moron. This jerk just proves that you can cover a pile of shit with diamonds, but when all is said and done, you still have a pile of shit!

"So tell me, Mr. Brewer...."

"Hey, please call me Ben. Both of you."

"Okay, Ben, what is your article about?"

"Well, Jack, is it okay if I call you Jack?" Jack starts to nod yes, and the reporter just keeps talking anyway, not even waiting for a response. I am really beginning to dislike this guy!

"I'm doing an expose really. With the crime rate going higher than it's ever been in Philadelphia, I want to give our readers an insight into what the police department is really doing about it. I mean are you guys actually out here fighting crime, or do you just drive around

8

all night eating and bullshitting. The people of Philadelphia have a right to know where their tax dollars are going, and what the police are doing about all of the crime in their backyards." I could hear Jack let out a small growl, he hates this guy as much as I do. This is going to be a long three nights!

I decide to take the ball back in my court, or Jack might blow. His fuse tends to be even shorter than mine.

"Well, *Ben*, I think you'll find that we do everything in our power to protect and serve the people in this great city of ours, and we do our best with *your* tax dollars. I'm proud to be an officer in the Philadelphia Police Department, we are some of the best. We are on a limited budget, but we do pretty damn good with what we have."

"Very nicely said, Officer Murphy. Is that in the policemen's handbook or do you actually believe that?"

I couldn't believe this guy, I've only known him for fifteen minutes, and I am already really hating him. I turn my head to look back at him and give him a piece of my mind, but then the radio squawks. Just in time to save him from one of my rants. The dispatcher is calling us.

"Car 63. Car 63. Come in." I am happy to answer the call, I won't have to deal with this asshole for now.

"This is car 63. Go ahead."

"We have a 420 in the alley behind Brookes Bookstore at 13th and Locust."

"Who called it in?"

"A female caller by the name of Maria Jacobsen. She lives in the apartment above the bookstore, she's waiting there for you."

"Roger. Car 63 responding." I switch on the siren and off we go.

"So what's a 420 guys?" Jack has cooled down enough to speak now. I am still pissed.

"It's a body."

"So I guess I'm really going to see some action after all." I am beyond disgusted at this point.

"Let me remind you again, Mr. Brewer, when we arrive at the location, you will stay in the vehicle."

"Well you're just taking all of the fun out of this, Officer Murphy, and its Ben, remember?"

"This is not supposed to be fun, Ben. It's a dead body in an alley. We have rules, if you cannot follow those rules, we will be happy to take you right back to the station after this call, is that understood?"

"Yes, Officer Murphy. Hey, Jack, is she always this much fun?" He said that in such a mocking tone, I just want to smack the shit out of him!

I am really fuming now, and Jack's blood pressure must be soaring. His face is beet red, and that little, tiny vein on his forehead is about to burst. This guy will be lucky if he gets back to the station, without me or Jack shooting him! Just as Jack and I are both about to tell this ass off, we whip into the alley, and our headlights shine right on the body.

The alley was dark, except for one overhead light that is hanging right over the corpse. If someone was trying to hide anything, they picked a shitty place to do it. As Jack and I get closer we can see it is the body of a young woman. Mid to late twenties, she is dressed in a long black gown. Her skin is so white, that under the light, it almost looks translucent. Her lips and fingertips look blue, and there is a dried trickle of blood coming from the corner of her mouth and the bruised puncture wounds on her neck.

Her arms are folded across her chest, and in her left hand she is holding a blue rose. The color matches her lips. This body wasn't just dumped here, she has been placed here... almost lovingly. Someone wanted her to be found, that was obvious.

Jack and I share a look, and we are both thinking the same thing. We knew this day would come, but I guess we were also hoping that it never would.

"We'd better call homicide right away, Jack"

"I'll get it Murph, and I'll get a statement from the lady who called it in."

"Great, I'll take a look around the alley." Jack puts his hand on my shoulder and gives a quick reassuring squeeze.

"Be careful, Murph."

I start to slowly look around the body, and the alley for any evidence. I hear footsteps, and a gasping noise, I pull my gun and turn around quickly. I have my gun pointing at the reporter.

"Oh God, she's dead. She's so young and so pale, so…."

"What the hell are you doing?! Get back in that car right now!!" I am shrieking at him. He has really crossed a line now. He just keeps staring at the dead girl, as if he's in a trance. He puts his hand over his mouth, and he starts to turn green.

"Get out of here right now, don't you dare throw up. This is a crime scene, get back to the car now!" I don't even wait for him to leave, I grab his arm and pull him back to the squad car.

"Don't you dare get sick in that car either, if you're going to be sick, there's a trash can right over there. What the hell were you thinking?!" With that he lost it, and lost it, and lost it some more.

Jack comes out of the apartment building and right over to us.

"What the hell is going on over here?"

"This jerk almost got his head blown off by coming into the alley and surprising me."

"It would've served him right if you had. Hey, we gave you strict orders buddy, you stay in the car do you hear me?" Ben is coughing and catching his breath. Jack grabs his arm and turns him around.

"Do you hear me?"

"Yeah, I mean, yes sir. I hear you."

Jack has a way of commanding respect. He's a big man, over six feet tall and muscular too, in his early fifties, silvery streaks in his hair. He has a booming voice, even when he's trying to be quiet.

With that we hear multiple sirens and a detectives' car comes screeching onto the street in front of us. Two men in suits get out of the car slowly and walk up to us. They look vaguely familiar, but I don't remember them well enough to recall their names. The taller of the two speaks to us while his partner goes into the alley to look at the body.

"I'm Detective Mills, that's Detective Harrison. So you two are the first on the scene, I take it?"

"Yes, I'm Officer Murphy. My partner

Officer Dunbar and myself just arrived a few minutes ago."

"Who's your friend?" He nods toward the reporter.

"Oh, he's just a ride along."

"I thought so from the look on his face." He seems to get a kick out of the sick look on Ben's face.

"Did you bag anything from the alley?"

"No, I'm sorry. I started to check the alley for evidence, while Officer Dunbar questioned the caller. But I was *interrupted*, and didn't get to finish looking."

I shoot the reporter a hateful look. The second detective had come back in time to hear his partner question me. They look at each other with snide grins on their faces and Detective Mills snorts a stifled laugh when he speaks to me.

"Uh huh, well we've got it covered now. You can go." He speaks so dismissively, as if he's talking to a rookie…a female rookie. In this line of work, that's as bad as it gets. I feel so humiliated and angry, I just want to get out of here.

Jack speaks up, he knows what I'm feeling, and he knows I just want to leave.

"The lady over there is Maria Jacobson, she lives in the apartment above the bookstore. She was walking her dog, and the dog kept straining to go into the alley, she looked that way and saw the body. She ran back up to her apartment and called 911. She says she didn't hear any noise in the alley all evening. She'd like to get back upstairs, I told her you might want to talk to her."

"Yeah, we'll question her, but I don't think she'll be of any help." Detective Harrison speaks for the first time.

"This is the third victim we've found like this in the last two weeks. Blue rose, black gown, in an alley under a light. The same damn puncture wounds in the neck, completely drained of blood. Of course never any witnesses or evidence either."

I open the back door for the reporter, and I climb into the front. I don't say anything further to the detectives. Jack mutters something to them and gets into the car. I am seething, but I wait until we pull away, and I turn to look at the idiot in the backseat. He is still holding his stomach.

"You know what *Ben*?" I say his name with every ounce of venom I have in me. He looks at me, startled.

"Yes Officer Murphy?"

"You want to know why I'm a cop? I'll tell you why. I grew up in a cop family, my father was a cop, my grandfather, and his father before him. Not to mention dozens of uncles and cousins too. This is a way of life in my family, and I am proud to put on this uniform every night. I love feeling like I'm keeping the streets where I grew up safe, and protecting people. But you want to know something else? Out of all those cops in my family, I'm the only female officer. I have had to work ten times harder than any of them did to get the same respect, and by you interfering in my job back there tonight, you just set me back in the eyes of those two detectives." The reporter is looking at me as if he's in shock.

"I, I, didn't mean any harm."

"Well you may not have, but not only did you interfere with my job, and make me look bad in front of fellow officers, you have been a complete ass tonight. You directly disobeyed our instructions. Did you even stop to think that someone could've been in that alley with a knife or gun, and you could've gotten hurt or killed? Or worse yet, by protecting you, you could've gotten me killed??!!! You stupid, idiot…" I have so much more I want to say, to call him, but Jack reaches over and touches my arm and tries to talk as quietly as he is capable of.

"Enough, Micki." He always calls me by my nickname when he is being my fatherly friend, and not just my partner.

I grab my arm away and fold my arms across my chest. I am still upset, and just need to cool down. I think the reporter is actually shell shocked, he doesn't seem able to speak for a moment. When he does attempt to talk, I turn to look at him again, and he looks positively sad. It almost makes me feel bad for yelling at him like I did. Almost, but not quite.

He speaks slowly and distinctly.

"Officer Murphy, I am so sorry that I endangered you, and well, myself too for that matter. I guess I just wasn't thinking. But that was no excuse to humiliate you or cause you any harm in front of those detectives. I would like to apologize to both of you for my behavior tonight. You are right, I've been a complete ass." He really looks like he means what he said, but I'm still not sure about him.

He continues to speak, and does sound sincere.

"You see, I'm very passionate about what I do too. I've dreamed of being a writer my whole life. I also feel like I am doing a service with my job, I am trying to get a weekly column. I really feel like I could do even more good with that. So my plan was to get this assignment, and come out here and catch me some bad ass cops who didn't give a shit. Maybe I'd get my gift of a column handed to me after my scathing report on the inadequacies of the Philadelphia police force. Hell, maybe even get a book deal out of it." He continues as we listen to him intently. I feel drawn into every word he is speaking now.

"After seeing that body… that poor girl…like *that*, well, it all became very real to me, and I realized this is life and death out here. This isn't a game, not some great way to get my name on a column. So, Jack and Officer Murphy, I do apologize, I am really beginning to see how wrong I was. I have behaved like a jerk and a stupid idiot, as you so aptly called me Officer Murphy. So, I hope you can both forgive me, and allow me to continue riding with you for the next couple of nights? I promise to obey your rules and be more respectful too."

"You can call me Micki." I hate to admit it, but his apology did get to me. It seemed very heartfelt, and I'm willing to give him another chance.

Jack looks at me and then into the rearview mirror at Ben.

"Are you going to do exactly as we tell you to do from now on?"

"Yes sir, Jack. I don't think I have the stomach to disobey ever again." He smiles then, and wow what a gorgeous one at that! He really looks like he has stepped right off of a magazine cover!

"So, what do you think Murph, should we keep him?"

"Oh, I guess. As long as he knows, that the next time he steps out of line, or out of this car, he's history!"

"Yes, Offi...I mean Micki, I understand that completely." Jack smiles at me, he approves.

We continue patrolling and thankfully the rest of our shift is uneventful. A car alarm going off, someone thought they heard a shot outside of their window, the usual.

Ben didn't ask too many questions the rest of the night, I think he's still a little queasy. He hasn't even attempted to get out of the car anymore either. I think he's very happy when our shift is over and we return to the station. But then again so am I.

Chapter Two

Jack and I go into the station house after saying goodnight to Ben. We stop to check in with the night clerk for a few minutes, the front door opens and in walks Ben.

"Jack, Micki, boy am I glad you two are still here. My car won't start. I just replaced the battery last week, so it can't be that. I would just call AAA, but my phone doesn't seem to be working either right now. So do you think one of you could help me out? " Jack and I look at each other, I know the last thing he feels like doing is messing with this. He just wants to get home to Betty, and get some sleep.

"I'll take care of it Jack, why don't you finish up things here and go home. I'll see you tonight."

"You sure Micki?"

"Yep, no problem. Say hi to Betty for me."

"Will do, be careful, and make sure he doesn't get out of line." I smack him on the arm and head out the door with Ben.

"So do you know about cars, Micki?"

"Nope, not a thing. I'll just drive you home, and then you can arrange to have someone come look at your car later today."

"You're a lifesaver. Thank you."

We get to my car quickly and after I start the car I realize I don't know where I'm taking him.

"Okay, where do you live Ben?"

"On Warnock St."

"You live in South Philly?"

"Yeah, is that too far? I can call a cab."

"No, no that's fine, but do you mind if we stop by my place first? I live a couple of blocks from here and I am dying to change my clothes, and I have to feed Isabella." He gives me a sudden, questioning look.

"You have a child?" His voice has a tone of sadness in it.

"I mean, well, I thought, that you were single?" He is slightly stammering. I can't help but smile and chuckle a little.

"No, no, Izzy is my cat. She's the closest thing to a daughter I'll ever have. Oh, and you are right Ben, I am single." It feels good for the mood to be easier, and lighter. The night had been so bad, this felt much better.

"Oh, yeah that's fine. Take as long as you need." He almost seems embarrassed. I take a little enjoyment in that too.

I don't know why I had just assumed that he lived near the station. South Philly isn't a long drive from here, but a little longer than I expected, and I want to be comfortable. Plus, Izzy gets very cranky if she's not fed on time.

Within minutes we arrive at my apartment. It feels good to be home, even if it is just for a minute or two. This is my down time, and I look forward to relaxing and just being myself. Plus, I wouldn't mind getting to know this Benjamin Brewer just a little bit better.

"Do you want to come in, I won't be long?"

"Yeah, it might be nice to see how a real police officer lives. I might be able to use some of this in my piece."

"Well I don't think you'll see anything that interesting, but sure, come on in."

Just as I expected, the minute I open the front door, Izzy is sitting there waiting for me. Purring her delight at the thought of getting fed on time!

"Hi my little baby, mommy's home. Are you hungry?" I get a very loud meow at that question! A resounding yes in cat talk.

"Well, this must be Isabella. Hi little kitty,

how are you doing?" Izzy is thrilled with the additional attention she is getting and starts wrapping herself all around Ben's legs, a greeting which she normally only reserves for me. It seems as though she approves of our visitor.

I take my shoes off and put my gun and shield away, so I can get to the urgent matter of feeding Izzy.

Ben looks around slowly and then follows me into the kitchen. Izzy leaves Ben's side the minute she hears food dropping into her bowl.

"This is really a nice place you have here. It's so open and airy, especially for being right in the middle of the city. I'm impressed."

"It's fairly big, especially for just me. But I like my space. In case you haven't noticed, I'm not very conventional. I love these old converted brownstones, so when this one went on the market, I grabbed it up. One thing you'll find out about me, is when I see something I want, I go for it."

"So has there ever been a Mr. Murphy?"

"Nope, and there never will be. The only Mr. Murphy I know was my father. I was pretty rebellious and wild as a teenager, and I guess part of me doesn't want to ever lose that freedom."

"So you think getting married would take away your freedom? It doesn't have to be that way, you know."

"You speak like you have experience in that matter?" For some reason I had just assumed he was single, but a man this good looking is most likely taken.

"Oh, so there is a Mrs. Brewer then?"

"Oh no, no. I've never been married either. I just meant that I've seen couples, well, people…" He is absolutely stammering now. He takes a breath and starts again.

"I guess what I'm trying to say is it depends on the couple, that's all."

"Maybe. I've just never seen that for myself. It just seems like it changes too many things, and I don't like compromise. Plus, I have never seen a truly happy couple stay that way."

"What about your parents?"

"My parents died thirteen years ago. They had started out happy enough I guess, but by the time they died they had been arguing almost constantly, and had even stopped speaking to each other"

"I'm so sorry to hear that. How horrible for you. How did they die? A car accident?"

I hadn't spoken of my parents in so long, it felt odd, as if I had never had parents. Thinking about them, and the way they died…I couldn't think about that. The only way to keep the horror of that night out of my mind was to never think about them or discuss them. The sadness and terror must be starting to show on my face, even though I had put my head down as I was speaking. But Ben sees something, because he starts to come closer to me, reaching out to put his hand on my shoulder. I move back suddenly. If he touches me right now, I will start to cry, and I haven't cried for my parents in a very long time. He stops suddenly, he must have gotten the hint.

"I am so sorry Micki. I didn't mean to upset you." He looks heartbroken, as if he himself has caused me the terror of that experience.

"No, I'm okay. It's okay. I just don't like discussing it, if you don't mind."

"Of course. I understand completely." I need to change the subject as quickly as I can. I can't take those sad puppy dog eyes staring at me anymore.

"Well, I am never going to get you home at this rate. Have a seat, and I'll be right out. Help yourself to anything you want in the fridge."

I go into my bedroom as fast as I can and close the door. I lean back against it, and take a deep relaxing breath. I hate anyone feeling sorry for me, and at that moment, that's exactly what I know Ben is feeling for me.

The first thing I do is let my hair down. I have long, curly hair and love for it to hang loose. It's all a part of taking off the uniform, and being me at the end of my shift.

I throw on a comfortable pair of jeans and my favorite black t-shirt. A tour shirt from the last time Springsteen was in the area. I grab my sneakers, and join Ben on the sofa. The minute he sees me, a huge smile breaks out on his face.

"Wow, you are really beautiful! I'm sorry if that sounds sexist, I don't want you getting mad at me again, but you are stunning."

"As long as you don't ask me again why someone like me is a police officer, I'll take the compliment and just say thank you." I flop down next to him on the sofa.

"No, I will never make that mistake again, I promise."

"Okay, so my turn now."

"For what?"

"To play reporter and ask you some questions." He chuckles at me and smiles.

"Go right ahead, ask away!"

"Well, we've established that there is no Mrs. Brewer…"

"Well I wouldn't exactly say that…" I shoot him the same quizzical look that he had given me earlier about Izzy.

"No, I am permanently single, but there is a Mrs. Brewer…my mom." I swat him on the arm with the throw pillow. He puts his head back and laughs. Such a deep, throaty, sexy laugh. It is so nice to hear. I can't help but start laughing too. It feels so wonderful. It just honestly feels so damn easy and good to be sitting here with him right now, enjoying this moment.

"Sorry about that I couldn't resist. You should've seen your face, it was priceless! But seriously, my parents are who I was talking about earlier, you know, the ones who can make marriage work, but still keep their independence."

"Okay, so I'll bite, what's their secret?"

"I don't exactly know. All I know is that they have always had a very deep love and respect for each other. There is no jealousy, there is some *compromise* though." He then swats me on the arm with the throw pillow.

He makes me smile again. I seem to be doing a lot of that with him.

"Go ahead, I want more details about this perfect marriage your parents have."

"Well, no marriage is perfect. But they have always worked through everything. It was really great for me growing up and seeing that. It made me know that a good, no, a **great** marriage is possible. They have such a passion about everything in their lives, hell just about living even. They are passionate about each other and their work and me of course."

"But wait a minute, you said earlier that you are a permanent bachelor. So why is that if they inspired you so? Or are you just having too much fun with the ladies?" I said the last part jokingly, but am actually wanting to hear his answer.

"You are going to laugh so hard when I tell you my reason." He looks at me as if he's asking me to please not laugh at him.

"Of course I won't, I really want to know."

"I honestly don't think I'll ever find a woman like my mother. Independent, strong, her own career. But a loving, caring, soul mate at the same time. That's how my Dad sees her, and I would want to see the same things in a mate for myself. I've never felt anything even remotely close to that, and I refuse to settle for anything less. So, I'd rather just stay single. Okay, go ahead and laugh now, I know you want to."

"No, I really don't." I didn't either. He speaks about his mother and his parents' marriage with so much love and warmth, it would be impossible to laugh.

"Oh and about me having fun with the ladies, there hasn't been one in my life for a very long time, no one special for an even longer time. I would be up for grabs, if the right woman ever did come along." He looks at me at that very moment with such a wistful look on his face. I am hoping I am not imagining that look and what it just might mean. I am really starting to like Mr. Ben Brewer!

"So what do your parents do?"

"Dad is a scientist. He worked for a private lab for years. But got everything out of that job that he could. So he then started teaching. He still does. At Albright. Mom is kind of a famous writer. A novelist actually."

"Oh wait a minute, your mom isn't Brenda Brewer?? **THE** Brenda Brewer??"

"Yes, as a matter of fact she is. Are you familiar with her books?"

"Well, Mr. Observant Reporter, you didn't look around here very well did you?" I point directly across the room to the bookcase where my entire collection of Brenda Brewer books are. She is the ultimate romance novelist, and has been my favorite since I was a teenager.

"She has to be the best romance novelist in the world. I love her books."

"I have to admit, I've never read any of her stuff. She always says that Dad is her inspiration, so a little too much information about their love life for me. But she'll be honored that I had the pleasure of meeting such a big fan of hers tonight. But when do you find time to read?"

"Oh, you'd be surprised. I love reading so much, I always have. It's such a perfect escape,

you know. Sometimes I stay up all day reading."
There is that sad puppy dog face again looking
me straight in the eye.

"What are you escaping from, Micki?"

"The usual. Bad memories, a stressful job,
nightmares." It is getting too serious again. I
normally don't open up this easily around
people. But something about Ben is just pulling
everything out of me. He sure knows how to
break down every wall I have ever put up. Maybe
it's the reporter in him, but I have a feeling it is
something more than that. Something much
more.

"So where do your parents live?" I want to
get the topic off of me.

"They are in Lancaster. They live in a
beautiful, refurbished farmhouse. It has an old
barn behind the house. Like one of those you'd
see on a postcard. Kind of falling down, real
rustic. But beautiful. They have a pretty garden
too. That's Dad's favorite hobby. Well, that and
the Phillies." He can make me smile so easily. It's
been a long time since I've had anything to smile
about.

"Well, if your dad is a Phillies fan, then he's
alright with me. I love the Phils, I wish I could
get to more games."

"Great, I can hook you up. My dad has
season tickets, so maybe we can take in a game

sometime with my parents."

"That sounds wonderful Ben, I'd like that." I don't know what is happening here, but I am really looking forward to meeting his parents and going to that game. Normally I have one night stands. No deep conversations, no future plans. If they try to get too close, or seem to want more than a night or two, I get rid of them. But this is different somehow. I'd be scared of how I'm feeling right now, if I wasn't so damn comfortable with him.

"You mentioned tonight that you've always wanted to write. Is that because of your mom?"

"I've wanted to write for as long as I can remember. I guess you could say that Mom encouraged me. She started reading to me before I was even born. Dad used to tell me she would lay in bed every night and read to her belly. Whole books. Would put him right to sleep. They both swear that I practically came out reading. Of course they will be happy to brag about that when they meet you." I smile brightly.

"So when did the writing start?"

"I truly don't remember when I first picked up the pen, but I wrote about everything and anything. I really got the bug though in high school and then got even more serious about it as a career in college. I've written everything. News reports, short stories, you name it. But my dream is to be a novelist. I want to write the great American novel someday. If I can get the column I want, it will give me more experience, lead me to some great contacts, give me the time and money I need so I can devote my life to writing the novels that I want to write. Who knows, maybe in the meantime, I may even be able to do some good with my column. I just want to make a difference, like you, just in a slightly different way."

When he talks about his writing he speaks with such passion, there is so much life and energy in his eyes. He is even more handsome, as if that were even possible. His eyes are sparkling and dancing, his voice and mannerisms are more animated, he has so much excitement for his life. I can no longer help myself, I lean over and kiss him on the mouth, hard. I think I took him by surprise, but then he responds in kind and kisses me back just as hard.

My hands are on his head, I'm grabbing his hair, and pulling him even harder into my mouth. I want him, I've never been so consumed with passion, I feel like I am on fire, and there is only one way to put it out.

He wraps his arms around me, and pulls my whole body to him. Our kissing is hot and passionate, almost frantic. It's as if we have both been starving, and we are each other's salvation.

I take my hands out of his hair just long enough to get his leather jacket off of him, and I rip his shirt from his chest. The buttons go flying, and so does his shirt for that matter. He quickly pulls my t-shirt up over my head, and throws it across the room, he sits there just staring at my breasts. Thankfully my bra had come off with my uniform!

He has the most incredible look on his face. He definitely likes what he sees. He slowly runs his tongue across his lips. The look in his eyes is pure hunger, and with one swift move he latches onto to the left one, and just lingers there… kissing, licking, and sucking. All the while he's caressing the right one. Squeezing and rolling my nipple with his long wondrous fingers.

My whole body is responding to his touch, his tongue. Just when I think I am going to explode, he moves his mouth to the right one, teasing the left one now, with just a fingertip.

That is all it takes for my entire body to feel complete arousal. My back is arching and I am lacing my fingers in his hair, pulling him against me as hard as I can. I want to get even more of me in his mouth. But I want more of him too, urgently. I need to feel him, all of him, against me, inside of me. With all of the willpower I have I pull my rock hard nipple out of his mouth, lock my lips on his and lead him up off of the sofa, and into my bedroom.

We are still kissing as I back him up to the bed. I break away from his lips long enough to unbuckle his belt and slowly, so teasingly slowly, I unzip his jeans. As I take my time pulling his jeans down, I keep rubbing the huge bulge that has developed. I yank his pants all the way off and throw them across the room. Oh, to my very pleasant surprise, he's commando! Got to love a man with easy access. Our lips find each other yet again, and there is no separating them this time.

He is more than ready for me. I can feel his hardness throbbing in my hand. He is keeping his hands quite busy too. They are rubbing and caressing my ass, finding their way inside of my jeans, sliding his fingers up and down my crack. He removes his mouth from mine just long enough to kiss his way down the front of my body, as he slides off my jeans and my thong. His tongue finds my wet, pulsing, sweet spot, and he latches on with his mouth. I am pushing myself into him as hard as I can, and with my fingers tangled in his thick hair I am pulling him with all my might, pushing his tongue, his lips, and his whole incredible mouth into me as hard as I can. I spread my legs and arch for him to get an even better taste of me, and as he keeps one arm behind my back to help support me, the fingers on his other hand have started doing their magical part, and before I know it, I am rocking back and forth, helping him to thrust his tongue deeper inside of me.

"Oh, Ben…oh, Ben….that's it, oh yes, Yes, YES…OHHHHHHHHHH." I feel as if an electrical current is racing through me as I cum. I am full of energy and my lust is even hungrier. Ben gives those lips one last kiss, and he smiles a devilish little smile at me as he kisses his way back up my body. He is taking great pleasure in my ecstatic state. I can see the same hunger in him that I am feeling.

We kiss again, white hot kissing, I want more of him, so much more. I throw him onto the bed, and I can't help but stare at him in all his glory. Of course my hungry eyes go right to his rock hard, pulsating, dick. I swear I can see the blood coursing through his veins, and see him growing even larger with every passing second. I keep my eyes on the prize as I swiftly land my mouth on it, licking it slowly up and down, and all around, just like a delicious, cream filled lollipop. Ben is already moaning and starting to pitch his body up, needing to find his way into my mouth. I am so hungry for him, I just have to taste him. I wrap my lips around his head and slide all the way down, and back up and back down again. My hands have found their way under him, and I am kneading, and rubbing his tight, round ass, as I suck him. His hands are wrapped in my hair, the curls laced around his fingers, and he is pulling me down on him even further and further. I love the feel of his long, thick, cock inside of my mouth, my throat. As I feel the heat and pulsing increase to a fevered pitch, as he groans and screams out my name, I suck him dry. Just as I suspected he would be, he is incredibly delicious.

He is panting, and smiling, as I slowly move my body up to lay beside him.

"You are amazing, absofuckinlutely amazing."

"You are pretty fucking amazing too, and your body is incredible, especially that one particular creamy centered part." He turns on his side to face me, and he is simply glowing, and I can feel myself glowing too. I have been with many men, but never have I felt so much passion, hunger, and heat before. We are smiling at each other, our faces only inches apart. Our arms across each other, and we kiss. Soft, tender kisses. He kisses me sweetly on my nose, and each cheek, and my eyelids. He is being so playful, I am wanting him even more. I kiss his upper lip, and his lower lip, and I am feeling his lust growing against my body. Our playfulness is becoming passionate and the heat is building once more.

We have our arms wrapped around each other, and seem to have found ourselves fondling and caressing each other's asses. Then our hands are moving all over each other. Rubbing, and tracing our fingers up and down our hot, sweaty bodies. Our tongues are thrusting, but we both are wanting more. *Needing* more. It's as if our bodies belong together, and never truly knew what passion was until this very moment. It feels like our body temperatures have risen to well over a hundred degrees. We are in an animalistic frenzy. What started out as playful kissing, and soft caresses, has turned into heated grabbing, sweaty clutching, pulling of hair, hardcore sex! I am pinching and grabbing his ass cheeks, biting his lips. He is squeezing my breast and pinching my nipple. He runs his tongue down my neck, and as he starts to bite, that's when I lose it completely and push myself down on him hard, so that his enormous shaft fills me.

The look on his face is full of sheer pleasure, and he is groaning slightly. A soft, deep growl coming from his sexy mouth. I want to hear him screaming out in ecstasy before our time together is over. We are thrusting in perfect rhythm. My whole body is quivering with electricity. We thrust slowly, and fully, so I can feel the full length of him each and every time.

Slowly in and slowly out. Slowly in, slowly out. As the wanting and groaning increase, so does our pace. Quicker and faster, quicker and faster, and all at once, he pushes his body up off of the bed to arch perfectly with mine, and with one last final thrust, I feel him exploding inside of me. We both scream out at the same time, and words will never be able to describe the incredible, indescribable, purest pleasure, that has completely taken over our bodies.

We shake and tremble and I just fall limp and exhausted on top of him. We wrap our arms around each other, and just stay fused together for as long as possible. We are breathless and motionless for a long time, and when we are finally able to open our eyes, we look deeply into each other's and then drift off to sleep.

I open my eyes when I hear the shower running. I look at the clock on my nightstand and three hours have passed. Just then, Ben comes out of the bathroom wrapped only in a towel and he smiles at me. I am so very glad that it wasn't all just a dream.

"Well hello there sexy. You slept well?"

"Oh hell yes, and how about you?" He walks toward my side of the bed.

"I slept very well, I feel like a new man. I had some wonderful dreams too."

"Hmmm, was anyone I know in them?"

"Oh yes, I do believe you just might know her. I didn't really know her until three hours ago, but I sure am glad I know her now." With that he leans down and kisses me softly on the lips.

"Mmm, I am so glad you know her now too." I am actually feeling slightly shy this morning. I am feeling things I don't want to feel, have never planned on feeling, knowing it just wouldn't be fair to the other person.

He interrupts my deep thoughts with another kiss, a deeper and more passionate one. I want him so much, all over again. It would be so easy to just take him in my arms right at this very moment, and we could ravage each other. But I have to think clearly right now. I have so much I have to look into today, after the events of last night. I cannot allow myself to get attached to anyone, ever. It would be so easy to do just that with him. But no, I can't.

I take my arms from around his neck, where they seem to just naturally go, and I place my hands on his chest and gently push him away. He looks stunned and then hurt. I speak quickly as I sit up and start getting out of bed.

"I really need to get in that shower myself, get dressed and then get you home. I have to go to the station and check on some things."

He backs away, and even though I thought I

had made a reasonable excuse, he still looks surprised.

"Is everything okay, Micki? I mean, did I do or say anything wro…" I immediately cut him off, I don't dare want him to think for one second that our passionate time together wasn't the most incredible experience of my life.

"Oh no Ben, no, believe me you did EVERYTHING right. It was amazing. **You** are amazing. This truly has nothing to do with you. I just really do have so much to do today, and if I don't stick to my plans, I'll stay in bed with you all day, and won't even feel like going anywhere."

We walk towards each other and my hands can't help but rub his chest. What an incredible six pack! His hands always seem to find my ass. Of course we kiss, deeply and passionately. We stop before there is no stopping.

"I, personally wouldn't mind that at all, I'd even be willing for just a little encore before I leave. A nice way to start your day?!"

There was that sexy little crooked smile that makes my blood go white hot and course through my veins…but no, I can't give in, not right now. I don't want to tell him what I'm really thinking. Sex with him was incredible, it was unlike anything I'd ever experienced before, and I've had some really great experiences. But that kiss just now was different. It had feeling in it, and I don't want that. I don't want a boyfriend, or a life mate. I just want hot, passionate sex. At least that's what I have always told myself. I can't ever allow myself to want more, not even with somebody as wonderful and perfect as Ben. I don't want a relationship, I just want a good screw! That's all I can ever have. I have resigned myself to that

"As tempting as that sounds, I just can't. How about a rain check?" I head for the bathroom before there can be any further discussion.

"Of course you can. I am counting on it."

"If you're hungry, help yourself to whatever you can find in the kitchen while I'm in the shower."

"Well I was hungry for something else, but I guess I'll have to settle for some food instead." I give him a smile and a wink, and close the bathroom door. I lock it too just in case he has plans on surprising me. As much as I would love that, I need to keep a clear head.

Coming out of the bathroom, I hear him on the phone.

"Thanks a lot Jim, I appreciate it. See you in a few." He hangs up and comes into the bedroom as I'm brushing my hair. I am almost sad to see him fully dressed.

"In case I forgot to tell you last night, your hair is beautiful. In fact everything about you is beautiful." He starts running his fingers through my hair, his touch feels incredible. I feel tiny electrical sparks with each stroke.

"Thank you. You're not so bad yourself." I can see his reflection smiling at me in my mirror.

"I called my friend Jim to come pick me up, so you can get everything done without worrying about taking me home."

"You didn't have to do that, I really don't mind."

"Actually, Jim drives a tow truck, so he'll take me to my car, and take a look at it. If he can't fix it, it has to be towed anyway, so it's just easier this way."

I get up from my vanity table and stand as close to him as I can. I just want, no I need, to be near him. To feel his breath on my face, smell the sexy scent of his freshly showered skin. I smile as I run my fingers down the front of his shirt where the buttons *used* to be.

"Uh, sorry about that." He looks down to see what I am talking about, and then smiles too.

"Oh, I'm not sorry at all."

I reach up and give him a quick kiss on the lips. He puts his arms around my waist and pulls me even closer to him and kisses me softly, tenderly, and deeply. Our tongues find each other once more, and there is that feeling again, a warm tenderness mixed in with the heat and passion.

A horn blowing in front of the house, suddenly distracts our kissing. Thankfully, because I don't think I could've resisted much longer.

"Damn, Jim has bad timing." I was thinking something more along the lines that we were saved by the bell…or horn, in this case.

"Yeah, you almost got your way." He really did too.

"Mmm, I could tell."

"I'll walk out with you, I just need to grab my keys and my yoga mat."

"You take yoga classes?"

"Three times a week."

"That definitely explains the limberness!" I give him a light smack on the ass.

We walk over to the tow truck, he grabs my hand and gives it a squeeze. He opens the passenger door, and we lean down slightly to look inside.

"Jim this is Micki, Micki this is Jim."

"Well hello there lovely lady. How are you doin'?"

"Hi Jim, I'm just fine thank you. Nice to meet you."

I'm not much for small talk, so I stand upright and Ben follows my lead. I place my hand around his neck, and kiss him softly on the lips. I love feeling his luxuriously thick hair in between my fingers. One kiss turns into two which turns into three. Finally we just giggle a little, and pull away from each other.

As I turn to walk away, he pulls me close one more time, and he kisses me sweetly on my forehead.

"Go get limber." He winks at me as he playfully swats my ass.

If I were looking for a man in my life, I could really get used to this one!

Chapter Three

I wasn't going to bother with my yoga class, there's too much on my mind. But it relaxes me, and clears my head. I need to keep things as normal as possible right now. Routine is good.

After my class, I head to the station. Everything about that body last night is still bothering me. It also bothered me when the detective said that this was the third one that had been found in the same way in the last two weeks. Why hadn't I heard about the other ones?!

When I walk into the station, I'm only slightly surprised to see Jack talking to a couple of plainclothes.

I tap him on the shoulder. He looks minimally surprised to see me too. He thanks the two detectives, and turns around to face me directly.

"So what brings you in here so early today, Micki?"

"The same thing that brought you in here so early too."

"Yeah, I had a feeling I'd see you here this morning after that girl last night."

"You better believe it. I can't understand why we haven't heard about the other two bodies. Something is wrong and I don't like it."

"Yep, that's exactly what I was thinking. Those two I was just talking to, gave me some details."

"What did they say?"

"Let's go to the diner and talk."

"I'll meet you there in a few minutes. I just need to look up something real quick and make a phone call."

I find the paperwork that Ben had filled out last night, and got his cell number.

"Brewer here." He sounded so serious, it was cute.

"Hello Brewer, this is Murphy." I tried sounding just as serious, but I'm sure he could hear the playfulness in my tone.

"Micki! What a nice surprise. What's up?"

"I was just wondering if you wanted to grab something to eat before patrol tonight?" *Oh please say yes, please say yes…*

"I would love to, just tell me when and where and I'll be there."

"How about Wesley's Diner, about nine o'clock?"

"Sounds great! I'm looking forward to it. I'll see you then!"

"See ya. Bye."

"Wait a minute, Micki. Just one more thing, how was your yoga class?"

"It was great, I am very limber! Bye Ben." I tried to sound as sexy as I could. I hadn't planned on calling him, but I couldn't help myself. I can't stop thinking about him today, and I am hungry for him.

I find Jack at the last booth in the back corner of the diner.

"Hey Jack, did you order already?"

"Yeah, my usual." Usual for Jack meant two eggs, over easy, white toast, bacon, and a side of scrapple. He was so predictable, but in a partner that was a good thing.

The waitress notices me right then and comes over right away. I wave her off.

"Nothing for me, thanks." Jack and I share a smile. I'm just as predictable to him.

"Okay, what did you find out?"

"Apparently everything is being kept very hush, hush. They don't want this to get out like the last time."

"So, it is like *last* time?"

"It looks that way. Three women, so far, all in their mid to late twenties, the black gowns, the roses, and the blood draining. We both know what that means."

"Yes, I'm afraid we do. Do they have any leads?"

"No, they seem pretty clueless. Naturally, they aren't even looking at the past case for suspects, considering that the killer from back then is dead."

"Yeah, right, *dead*. But we both know that isn't quite the case." The waitress returns with Jacks' food.

"Thanks, Nancy."

"What is homicide thinking?"

"They are thinking it's a copycat, naturally. They are even looking in the department for a suspect."

"You don't mean the…"

"No, no, not the task force. They just don't know where else to look. There are never any clues, the cases are identical except for one thing, did you notice what that was last night?"

"Yeah, the hair. Last time they were all blondes, this time I'm assuming brunettes, since the girl from last night was."

"Yep, that's it. So they are thinking that maybe it's someone who either prefers brunettes or just isn't following every detail of the last murders."

"What are we going to do Jack?"

"They have interviewed some neighbors at the three crime scenes, and I want to get a look at those interviews, see if there's any mention of *him.*"

"Last time he really stood out."

"How about if we meet at the station early tonight, before that reporter shows up and go through some files?" Oops, how am I going to explain this one?!

"Actually, Jack, I kind of made plans with Ben tonight, here at the diner at nine." I'm not sure what my face looks like, but Jack definitely picks up on my apprehension, and a light bulb seems to go off over top of his head.

"Micki, what happened last night when you drove him home?" He sounds more like a disapproving father, instead of my partner.

"Nothing. A lot. Jack we've had this discussion before. What I do when I'm off the clock is my own business, as long as it doesn't affect you or my job. I'm a big girl, and it's my life, so no lectures!"

"You hated him last night. I was doing everything I could to keep you from shooting him, what the hell changed that?"

"You heard him after the blow up in the car. I

49

believe that he was sincere."

"Micki, you are playing with fire! You are gonna get burned one of these days, that's all I'm saying."

"I know, I know. But I can handle this. It's nothing serious, just a good time. It's not like I'm falling in love with him or anything. He's just a really nice guy and I enjoy his company. It's okay Jack, really. I can take care of myself. So don't worry, okay?" I don't know who I was trying to convince more…me or Jack.

"Okay, okay. Just please be careful!"

"I will, I promise." I added a big smile to ease his worry.

"Actually, I guess there's something good about this. If he's here with you, he won't be getting to the station early and causing people to look for us. Plus, it's probably better for just one of us to look through the files anyway, to avoid any questions."

"You're probably right about that, so now, *you* be careful! If this is anything at all like last time, you know those files are being watched carefully."

"You know, it's a damn good thing your reporter friend didn't pick up on what that detective said about this being the third body. We can't afford for this to get in the papers."

"Oh I think he was too busy being sick to

even hear what the detectives were saying. I'm sure he didn't catch on."

What I was actually thinking was that I think he stayed very pre-occupied through the morning with other things, to even remember anything about that dead body. I had to smile at that, remembering the morning myself, it sure felt amazingly good just thinking about it.

"Micki, did you hear me? What the hell are you thinking about with that big shit eating grin on your face?" I give him an even bigger smile…

"Wouldn't you like to know?"

"Oh, geez, no Micki, for Gods' sake I don't want to know!"

I couldn't help but laugh at him, he was so cute when he was acting disgusted with my behavior.

"Well, to get that thought out of my head, back to this case. I really should talk to someone on the task force, I guess."

"That's probably not a bad idea, and I know they kind of freak you out, but you know that I can't talk with them. They are even more disapproving of my life than you are."

"Well after last night, they may have a reason to disapprove!"

"Ha ha, very funny Jack."

"Okay, so it's a plan, you keep your *boyfriend* here, until it's time for you to come to the station, and I'll see what I can dig up."

"Okay, but he's not my *boyfriend*! He's just a really good fu…"

"Okay, okay, Micki, shut up!" He puts up his hand to make sure I stop right there, and he makes me laugh even harder this time. I love goofing with Jack when he's acting all fatherly. It's so much fun pushing his buttons.

It's almost nine, here I am back in this diner again. For someone who never eats here, I sure am here a lot. I don't normally worry about what I am wearing, but I found myself making a conscious effort to look good for Ben tonight.

I left my hair hang loose, he seemed to like that this morning. I even put on a little bit of makeup. That is something I hardly ever do. But some mascara and lip gloss can go a long way.

I decided to wear a tight pair of black leggings, very easy to get off. I know what I want tonight, there is no sense denying it. Instead of my usual t-shirt, I have on a long sleeve knit shirt, purple and black stripes, very form fitting and no bra tonight. My turn to go completely commando!

I'm just shy of being five foot two, a size one, I usually shop in the juniors section.

Most people never guess that I'm twenty-eight, everybody thinks I'm a teenager. Then when they find out that I'm a cop, they really have a hard time believing that.

I hate wearing shoes, especially my work shoes, they are so heavy. There is nothing like going barefoot. If I could, I'd just skip shoes all of the time, but I think people might question my sanity! Well, more than they already do. But tonight I decide on a pair of fancy black sandals, with just a small heel. Ben is almost six feet tall, so anything I can do to get closer to those incredible, kissable lips, I am willing to do.

The door swings open just then, and there he is. My body is already responding to the mere sight of him. I wave so he will see where I am sitting, and he smiles broadly as he comes towards the booth.

"Well, hello there sexy. You look beautiful tonight." He bends down and gives me a soft forehead kiss. I am struck breathless by the feel of his soft lips on my warming skin. I try to compose myself before he notices.

"Thank you, you are looking pretty damn good yourself."

He has on the same brown leather jacket from last night, and it looks so sexy on him.

"Well thank you. I'm sorry if you've been waiting long, I got busy doing some research, and lost track of time."

"I just got here a few minutes ago myself, so you're okay." Oh, he's definitely more than okay.

He is a gorgeous, sexy man, and he smells sooooooo delicious. I just want to jump right over this table and………

"Hi, I'm Linda, can I get you something to drink?"

"What would you like Micki?"

"Can I just get a glass of water with a slice of lemon, please?"

"I'll have the same, but with a slice of lime."

"Here are your menus, I'll be right back with your drinks." Neither one of us picks up the menus, I think we are both hungry for something besides food. At least I know I am.

The waitress is back with our glasses of water in record time.

"Thank you, this will be all for me." Ben looks at me only a little oddly.

"Nothing for me either, thanks."

"Ben, please get something to eat. I'm just not hungry. I ate a very late lunch at home, and I'm still stuffed."

"No, I'm not really hungry either. I was picking the whole time I was doing my research, and didn't even realize how much I had eaten, so I am full too. Anyway, I was just anxious to see you and talk to you."

"Me too. So what would you like to talk about?"

"Well, something occurred to me this

afternoon that I had forgotten all about this morning, and I had to check it out." He looks so excited, his eyes are sparkling and he just seems so, *exhilarated*. It's enjoyable seeing him like this.

"What would that be?"

"What that detective said last night, about the other two bodies." Oh shit he did hear that. Maybe I should've stayed in bed with him all day, and kept him occupied. I know I would've really loved that.

"What about it?"

"You weren't surprised by that? You looked so stunned."

"I am surprised that you even heard him as sick as you were, let alone knew what my expressions were."

"I'm a reporter, I hear everything, even when my head is inside a garbage can and I am puking my guts out." We laugh.

"But seriously, when it came to your expressions, well, I didn't take my eyes off of you all night. That had nothing to do with my being a reporter though."

"You are very sweet. Are you always this charming? You always seem to know the perfect thing to say."

"I have never been called charming before, that truly is a first. I think it must be you who brings it out in me….if that's what I am really being. Are you trying to change the subject by any chance?"

"No, I really am serious about you being charming Ben. As for the other bodies, I may be trying to skirt the issue a little. You are starting to venture into dangerous territory. But no, I honestly didn't know. Jack and I hadn't heard a thing about them."

"That's what I thought. I did some checking and found out about the other two bodies. They are identical to the one last night. Long brown hair, the gown, blue rose, everything. I even know where the other two bodies were found. One was in the alley behind Stampanos' Restaurant, and the second one behind Phillys' Coffee & Bagel on Broad."

"How did you find all of this out?"

"You are not the only one who has friends in blue." I hated officers who spilled their guts to the press.

"Jack did some checking too today and we discussed it earlier."

"So what did he find out?"

"Now you know I can't tell you that Ben!"

"I know, but I had to ask anyway, you know, the reporter in me."

"That's what I'm worried about. You cannot print this Ben, please. It would hinder the investigation, and it just causes a lot of unnecessary concern to the public. We start getting tons of crank calls, people swearing that they see a killer on every corner, and……"

"Relax Micki, no I'm not printing anything until it's the right time. You know that it's going to eventually get leaked to other reporters, and they'll jump right on it. I'm willing to wait a little while."

"It's just so important that this doesn't get out right now. I'm hoping that you understand."

"I do understand. I'll wait as long as I can, and I promise that I'll come to you first before I print anything, just so you're not taken by surprise."

"I appreciate that. So, can we talk about something else now?"

"Of course, what would you like to talk about?"

"Did you get your car fixed?"

"Yes, as a matter of fact I did. Jim towed it to his shop, it was just a minor fix. It's good as new. Why?"

"What kind of car do you have?" Ben looks at me, curiously, and answers haltingly. I know he must be wondering why I am asking about his car, of all things.

"I have a Ford Focus…why the sudden interest in my car?" He has the cutest look of confusion on his face. It is making me even hotter for him.

"Hmmm, smaller than mine."

"Yes, your Mustang is bigger…and why are we talking about our cars?"

"Just wondering who has the bigger back seat." All of a sudden the confused look is gone from his face, replaced by a devilish grin.

"Ohhh, I see! You definitely win that one."

"I know, lets' go."

I reach over as I start to stand up and grab his hand, it feels like an electric pulse going through both of us. He throws a ten dollar bill down on the table, and as we practically run out of the diner, he puts his arm around me and I can plainly see that my nipples aren't the only things that are rock hard.

As we leave, our waitress Linda, yells a big thank you. I bet that's the largest tip she's ever gotten for two glasses of water!

Thankfully, I had parked in the back of the diner, away from any lights or other cars. We can't keep our hands off of each other, and I especially like rubbing a certain part of him. I already have my keys out, and I open the back door. We jump in, laughing and giggling like teenagers. We start to kiss, and things change at that very second, we are no longer like teens thrashing about.

Our kissing is deep, passionate, and there is

something so serious about it this time, it keeps building. Building to something that I have never felt before. Not even like the time before. Something so incredibly wondrous is happening. It is unlike any yearning I've ever had for any man in my whole life. I can't be absolutely sure of course, but I think he is feeling the same way.

The monumental heat is rising, and we start getting breathless, our hands running along every inch of each other's bodies. We rip the clothes off of each other, they are getting in the way. The back seat is proving to be a little more difficult than I had anticipated, but we are managing, very nicely!

Laying back on the seat, with Ben on top of me. I throw one leg over the back of the front seat and the other one braced on the roof. He kisses me all over, and we start moving together, and as he slides all of himself deep inside of me, we both groan. Actually it is more of a growl, at the same time.

We smile at each other, and I wrap my legs around him tightly. As our bodies move more rhythmically, we are filled with even more heat and desire than before. The passion climbs to a height that I have never known was even possible. It feels magnificent, *he* feels magnificent. I feel as if I have been struck blind with pleasure. I'm unable to focus on anything but the pure, intense waves of passion that my whole body is experiencing.

We are both moaning and growling, louder and bolder. We are holding each other so tightly and close, not even a ray of light can get between us. Our hips are doing all of the work, grinding and thrusting. We are clinging so tightly to each other. It's as if we never want to let go, like we are holding on for dear life. Then, suddenly, all time stands still. It's as if our bodies are moving in slow motion, taking our time to feel each and every part of each other, inside and out. It's miraculous, magical, and beyond anything of this earth. It feels like our bodies have been one for a heavenly eternity.

The flames burn brighter still and we begin pounding faster and harder. My arms are actually starting to hurt from holding him so tightly, but the pleasure is so intense, euphoric. I start to silently cry. I have never felt this way before, never have I been so emotionally moved. Literally moved to tears. I don't know what this really is, but I don't ever want it to end.......

"OOOOOOOOHHHHHHHHHHHHH"

We both hoarsely scream out at the same time, and even after we have reached the very highest peak of ecstasy, we still can't let go of each other.

We stay completely joined, drenched in

perspiration, trembling and shaking, in the back seat of my car, melded together. A tear runs down my cheek, and it may have been a bead of sweat running down Bens', but something deep inside of me tells me it is a tear too.

Neither one of us speaks for a while. I don't think there are any words we can say, there are no words to express what we have just experienced.

Chapter Four

When we finally catch our breath, and the trembling starts to subside, when I feel that I am finally able to control my emotions again, I kiss him softly on his ear. He lifts his face to look at me, he has been crying too.

He smiles sweetly and lovingly at me, and kisses me on my lips. The kiss is warm, and gentle. So full of tenderness. I don't want our lips to ever part, but then reality starts to filter in, and I realize that I have forgotten all about work.

I finish our kiss and manage to lift up my arm to look at my watch. Exactly fifteen minutes to get to the station and get ready for my shift. I don't want to, but I have to move. Ben must be sensing the same thing and he speaks first.

"We have to get to the station now, don't we?"

"Yes, unfortunately we do." We both are barely speaking above a whisper. It's as if we are in a place of absolute wonder and beauty and don't want to ruin it with voices.

"Ben…" My voice starts to quiver, I guess I'm not completely in control of my emotions just yet after all.

"Yes, Micki?" His voice sounds just as shaky.

"I hate to have to go."

"Me too."

We are still holding each other. Ben starts to sit up. I have to say something more.

"One last thing Ben…thank you."

"For what?"

"For making me feel something that I have never felt before."

Damn it, I really don't want to get emotional, but I can't let this end without telling him that.

"Micki, I don't know what just happened here, but I've never experienced anything like that before either!" He strokes my face with his fingers, and kisses me one last time.

Even though I know I should be rushing, I am moving in slow motion. We both put our clothes on slowly, and I start to get out of the car to get into the drivers' seat. Ben grabs my arm, and when I turn to look at him, we kiss again. As our lips part, he smiles at me and winks.

"I'll meet you at the station."

"I'll be right there."

As he walks over to his car, I can't take my eyes off of him. What a gorgeous man, and what a tender, loving, sweet man too. He is so incredible in every way. How am I ever going to be able to let him go when the time comes?

He is already inside the station when I get there, he smiles at me the minute I walk in.

"Jack and I will be back shortly, I just need to change."

"Don't change too much, you're perfect just the way you are." I roll my eyes, and laugh at his corniness. Our hands brush against each other briefly. Sparks immediately start to fly, which has now become expected and much anticipated.

In the locker room, I change slowly. I just can't seem to get Ben and my sudden feelings for him out of my mind. I've never felt like this before. I've heard that this was possible, heard old wives tales, or that was what I had always thought they were. But never believed it was true, and if it was, that it would ever actually happen to me. But I can't deny what I am feeling, it is too overpowering to ignore.

I have to get control of myself, I'll worry about this later. Right now, I need to talk to Jack, and see what he found out today. We have a job to do, and I can't allow anything at all to interfere with that, ever. It would not only be dangerous to do so, but it could be deadly.

"Micki, are you in there?" Jack is knocking at the door.

"Come on in Jack." It must be later than I thought.

"I'm just pulling my hair back, I'll be ready in a sec. So what did you find out today?"

"Well I got a look at the files, not a whole lot to see. No suspects, no witnesses, no nothing. It's almost as if pages are missing from them." One immediate thought hits me, I'm sure Jack was thinking the same thing.

"Did you talk to the task force?"

"Not for long, they wouldn't see me for more than five minutes. Gave me some kind of runaround, saying that these cases are of no ones' concern but theirs, then telling me that I needed to make an appointment to talk to them in the future."

"Sounds like they are the same as ever."

"They asked about you Micki." That spun me around on my heels and I looked directly at Jack.

"What did they want to know?"

"Just asked how you were doing in your job, if I had any problems with you as a partner, and they did make something very clear." I have a bad feeling I already know what he is going to say even before he says it.

"They won't talk to me again without you!"

"Shit!"

"I thought you'd feel that way. Look, Micki, don't worry about it, we just won't talk to them. They probably won't tell us anything anyway. We can always talk to them later on if we need to."

"No Jack, it's important that we know what's going on. I figured they might want to talk to me again, it's been awhile."

"You sure, Micki?"

"If they don't like my way of life, they can kiss my ass!"

"Micki! With an attitude like that, you're only going to piss them off!"

"I'll behave Jack, I promise, okay?"

"You'd better!"

"So when do they want to see me?"

"They suggested that ten o'clock tomorrow morning would suit them."

"Oh really? Well, I'm hoping to be very busy tomorrow morning at ten, we'll make it two."

"I keep telling you that you're playing with fire kid. Sometimes you just don't use your head."

"I always know exactly what I'm doing Jack. You just don't always agree with it!"

"Speaking of that, how did things with your

reporter go tonight?"

I've never been accused of being shy in any way, but I immediately put my head down and start fiddling with my uniform. I can feel myself starting to blush.

"Fine. Perfectly fine!"

"Are you okay Micki?"

"Sure, why do you ask?"

"You just seem, oh, I don't know, different."

I compose myself, and look into Jacks' face once again.

"I am great Jack. Really. No need for any concern at all!" That is true, there isn't any need for Jack to be concerned, but I, on the other hand am scared to death.

"C'mon Jack, time to get to work, isn't it?" As we walk to the reception area, I fill Jack in on everything Ben had found out from his inside source. Ben is waiting near the front door for us.

"You ready to roll Ben?"

"Hi Jack, I sure am."

"Then let's get out of here."

Ben immediately walks over to be next to me, and I can feel his eyes all over me. I am starting to feel very warm and flushed, from head to toe. But quickly enough we are outside in the cool night air, and I feel like I can breathe again. Until I look at him. Every time I look at him I feel breathless all over again.

It's so very quiet in the squad car. Ben keeps staring at me, but I can't return his gaze. I need to keep my head together tonight, I have a lot of thinking to do about my meeting tomorrow, these latest murders, and I need to stay focused. That is becoming increasingly harder to do anytime I'm near him, or look at him, or think about him, or hear his voice, or smell his scent…oh, I have got to stop this. I have to concentrate, but all I can think of is making mad, passionate love to him again. Over and over again.

Thankfully, the radio breaks the silence, and my train of thought.

"Car 63. Car 63 come in."

"Car 63. Go ahead." I gladly take the call

"We have a 420 in the alley behind the Regalia Movie Theater on Franklin."

"Who called this one in dispatch?"

"Anonymous caller. A male voice with an accent."

"Make a copy of that tape, dispatch. It's evidence now."

"Yes, Officer, will do."

"Could you recognize what type of accent it was?"

"I was the one who took the call, he sounded Bavarian or German, or something similar."

"Roger that. Car 63 responding." Jack and I

immediately look at each other. We know what that means, and it is exactly what we were afraid of.

I turn and look at Ben. He's staring at me, and he looks very concerned. I know he noticed the look that Jack and I exchanged. So I give him a reassuring smile to let him know that everything is okay. No reason for him to have to worry. He has to be kept in the dark about some things and this is definitely one of them.

"Is everything okay? Is there some significance about the caller having an accent?" Jack jumps in and handles Ben's questions. He knows how much I loathe lying to the people I care about.

"Nope, nothing for you to worry about at all. We are just answering a call, doing our jobs. That's it, end of story." I knew Ben wouldn't be quieted that easily.

"I saw the looks on your faces after you got the call from dispatch. It definitely seemed like something is wrong. What does the accent mean?"

I jump in this time, I don't want Jack losing his temper and making Ben more inquisitive. Maybe I can calm his questions.

"Ben, really it's nothing. Please sit back, you should have your seat belt on. We'll be there any minute. You remember the rules right?"

"You bet, I promise. I'll stay right here, and won't get in your way."

"Thanks, Ben."

The car is quiet again as we speed to the scene. When we pull up, there is already another police car there. The two police officers are in the alley talking. They look familiar from roll call. I think their names are Henderson and Williams.

Jack and I get out of the car and walk over to where they are standing. As soon as they see me, they look horrified. Officer Williams, I think that one is Williams, turns a ghostly shade of white. Jack and I look at the officers, then each other, and since they weren't speaking, we walk past them, and over to where the body is.

Victim number four, same black gown, blue rose, under a light, but the bulb is very dim. I see the same puncture wounds on her neck, and then my eyes go to her face, and I immediately see why the two cops looked at me the way they did. She looks so much like me, we could be sisters! I look at Jack, and he is already staring at me.

"My God, Micki. She could be your twin."

"She does look a lot like me doesn't she?"

"A dead ringer. Shit, sorry about that, but you know what I mean."

"Yeah, I also know what this means. It's a

message for me."

"Now c'mon Micki, we don't know that for sure. Let's not jump to any conclusions yet."

"Jack, it's staring you right in the face, literally! We both know what this means. Don't try to protect me." Jack puts his head down. He knows that I am right, he just doesn't want to admit it.

"Well, whatever this means, it makes your meeting with them even more important tomorrow. Can't you postpone whatever you have planned for tomorrow morning, and see them at ten like they want?"

"No, they are not running my life, but I know it's even more important that I speak to them now, so I'll be there at noon, okay?"

"At least I got you to compromise a little bit, that's a start." There's that word again. But maybe some things are worth compromising a little bit for.

The other officers walk up to us and Officer Williams speaks directly to me.

"Hey, we are really sorry we reacted like that, but you've got to admit, you and her look identical. It just kind of freaked us out."

"It's okay, don't worry about it."
Jack seems very impatient, and doesn't want this bozo saying anything more to me. He's being fatherly again.

"Did you call homicide yet? If so, Officer Murphy and myself will get back on patrol."

"Oh, yeah, yeah sure, they should be here any minute. There's no need for the two of you to stay. We already scanned the whole area, and there's nothing here."

I know Jack wants to get me out of here. He would do anything to protect me, and I am very glad of that. I am trying to remain professional, but I am more than a little unnerved by this latest turn of events, and I am dreading the rest of this shift. I just want to forget all about this for a while. Turn my mind off. I don't want to face this right now. I just want to be with Ben. He's all I can think of. I just want him to hold me and make love to me. I honestly don't know now, how much longer we may have.

I start walking back to the squad car, and Jack stops me.

"Are you okay, Micki?"

"I'm fine. Just a little anxious, I really don't want to think about anymore of this right now, okay?"

"Okay, I understand. Just get your composure before we get back to the car. That reporter doesn't need to know any of this."

"You want to know something Jack? Ben is the only thing getting me through this right now. Being with him is the only thing holding me together at this minute."

As I walk away from Jack, and head for the car, I hear him quietly say…

"Oh shit."

I get into the car not saying a word to Ben, or even looking at him. Jack quickly follows.

"So what happened? Was it another one?" He is looking at me, but I can't answer him. He turns to Jack instead.

"Jack, what was it, what's wrong?"

"It's number four."

"Identical in every way to the other three?"

"Yep, identical." Jack looks at me, Ben's eyes follow.

"What's wrong Micki?"

"Nothing, I'm okay."

"Jack, what's wrong with her? What happened?"

"If Murph says she's okay, then she's okay. If I were you, I'd leave it alone."

I can hear the helplessness in his voice, and it's making me very sad. There are things I can never tell Ben, no matter how much I care for him. There will always have to be lies between us, and I hate that. I hate all the damn lies.

Jack calls into dispatch

"Dispatch. This is Car 63 leaving the scene of that 420 on Franklin. We are heading in with a medical issue, we'll need a patrol replacement."

"Roger that car 63, will notify headquarters."
I shoot Jack a hard look. He has never done that before, ever!

We have always stayed on patrol no matter what. That tells me that he is as nervous about all of this as I am. I don't like that!

"Will one of you please tell me what's going on? Does that mean that we are heading back to the station, and who has the medical issue? Are you okay Micki?" Jack jumps in to handle the situation for me.

"That's exactly what that means. She's fine, I'm the one getting a stomach bug. It's best not to be out on the streets when that hits, if you know what I mean. Besides, Murph and I haven't had a night off in two weeks, I think tonight is the perfect night for one. We have to be back at the station at noon tomorrow for an important meeting, and we need to be fresh for that, right Murph?"

"Exactly right. Let's go in."

I'm not thrilled that Jack is taking us in, it doesn't feel right. Neither one of us has ever missed a night of work. But, what the hell. We have no idea what tomorrow holds in store for us, and I want tonight to just be all mine...

Mine and Bens'.

Chapter Five

When we arrive at the station, I hate the thought of even going in, all I can think of is going home with Ben. Of course, I am being rather presumptuous, I don't even know if Ben wants to spend the night with me, but something tells me he does…

Jack goes in ahead of me. I think he can actually see what is happening between Ben and me.

"I'll meet you inside Murph."

"Okay, I'll be right there."

Ben and I stand outside of the car, and I'm not quite sure what to say. Should I just be direct and ask him if he wants to come home with me, or should I wait for him to ask me? Before I even have time to make a decision, Ben wraps his arms around me, and holds me tightly. His arms are my heaven. I just relax and melt right there inside his embrace. I put my arms around him, and hold onto him just as tightly. He lifts my face up to look at him.

"Look, I don't know what happened back there, but I know that something has you upset, and I'm just trying to let you know that I'm here for you. If you want to talk about it, or anything else, I'm not being a reporter right now. I'm being your, well, your...what am I anyway?" There's that big smile that I love so much.

"You are my, um, well, my very, very, very good friend."

"I think we can do better than that in time. Now, your place or mine?" All he has to do is look at me and I instantly feel as though I don't have a care in the world. Everything is perfect right now, in this moment, in my small little world, in his arms

"Well, my place is much closer." I smile just as brightly as he is.

"Why don't you go do what you have to do inside, finish up with Jack and I'll meet you at your place."

"Okay, sounds great. I'll see you in a little bit."

"I can't wait."

"Me either."

We kiss, it's sweet and warm. The minute he leaves, I am already longing to be back in his arms again. But that will have to wait. I need to get changed and see Jack before I leave.

I change out of my uniform as fast as I can. I brush through my hair, and try to make it look as good as I can.

Jack is waiting for me in the hallway. He has changed, and is ready to go home too.

"Hey, Jack. Thanks for tonight. I feel horrible that we came in early, but I couldn't stand one more minute out there."

"To be honest, neither could I. You know that I do worry about you."

"I know, and I love you for it. So, I'll see you here at noon?"

"You better believe it. I'm keeping a close eye on you now."

"I'll be fine."

"I know you will. I'm going to make sure of it. So where's lover boy?"

"Ben is going to meet me at my place. He's probably already there, so I'd better go. Thanks again."

"Not so fast, I'm walking you to your car."

"Let's not blow this out of proportion, besides I can take care of myself."

"I know you can, but I'm not taking any

chances with you. This is serious, and I want you to take it that way."

"Believe me, I am. That body tonight was a calling card. He's back to try to finish the job this time. I know that, and I know that you know that too! I'm not taking any chances with my life. I'm watching my back." We walked as we talked, and were at my car in no time.

"Maybe we can get some answers tomorrow, and get this taken care of fast, Micki."

"The sooner the better as far as I'm concerned." I kiss Jack on the cheek. He looks misty eyed for a moment.

"Get home kid, and make sure you don't go into your place alone."

"I won't. I'll be very careful. Now go home and spend some time with Betty. She'll be surprised to see you."

"As long as she's pleasantly surprised, I'm happy."

"Night, Jack"

"See you tomorrow, Murph."

"Yep, see you tomorrow."

Good, Ben is already here waiting for me. I do feel better not going into my house alone. He jumps out of his car and rushes over to open my car door for me.

"Hi, thanks."

"Hi, sexy. Here this is for you." He hands me

one of those tiny little fake roses that you buy at the gas station.

"Awww, thank you Ben. That is so sweet."

"I wanted to get you real roses, but I didn't realize how late it is, and the only store open is Wawa. Next time, I'm getting you a dozen roses in any color you want."

"Any color except blue." Ohhh bad joke. I don't want to think about that tonight. I **won't** think about that tonight.

"Enough of that. Let me see if I can make you forget all of the bad stuff from tonight." He bends down, places his hands gently on the sides of my face, and gives me the most amazing kiss. My lips immediately tingle in response. I instantly feel lightheaded, and my body is already trembling. I can barely remember my name, let alone anything else from tonight! I pull away, just for one second, to catch my breath.

"Are you alright Micki?" He has such a mischievous smile on his face.

"Oh, I'm better than alright. You just have a way of making me, and everything, feel perfect."

"Thank you for the compliment, but I don't do anything special you know."

"I beg to differ with that. Everything about you is very special."

"Well we could disagree about this all night, but let's get inside and talk about something else." I smile up at him and we walk to the door, our arms wrapped tightly around each other.

I don't ever want to let him go, I want to feel all of him close to me, next to me, on top of me, inside of me. I can tell he is feeling the same way. It isn't just his physical reaction to my nearness, which would be obvious to anyone looking at him.

No, it is almost as if I can read his mind, I know what he is thinking and feeling at any given moment, and the more time I spend with him, the stronger this "sense" is becoming. It is all so new to me, I have never felt this way about anyone before that I have been intimate with. I've never developed feelings for any of the men I have slept with. They were all just a good time, good sex and that was it.

This is all so very new and different for me. I am still not quite sure how I am really feeling about all of this, but I will analyze all of that another time. Right now all I can think about is getting inside with Ben, and ravaging him!

Chapter Six

He takes my key from my hand, and like the gentleman he is, he opens the door for me. Which leaves my hands free to roam all over his body, I especially enjoy rubbing a particularly huge bulge that has developed in the front of his pants. I am such a lucky woman!

Our mouths find each other again as we stumble through the front door. He winds his arms around me tightly and pulls me to him so closely. I do likewise, and turn him around as I kick the door shut with my foot. I push him against the door, hard, and as I am thrusting my tongue in his mouth, and unbuckling his belt, he places his hands on my shoulders, and gently pushes me back an inch or two. Isabella apparently finds all of this very uninteresting, meows once, and scampers to her bed.

I look at him, like a child who is about to have her favorite toy taken from her.

"Micki, wait a minute, I just want to do this right."

"Have we been doing it wrong?" I chuckle.

"Definitely not, but I want us to take our time. I'm just speaking for myself, understand. But I am feeling so much more for you than just lust, although that is definitely strong too. I think you are feeling the same way about me, at least I hope you are. I want to make mad, passionate love to you, slowly, all night long, over and over again. I want to kiss and touch and explore every inch of your incredible body. I want to know you more intimately than I've ever known any other woman in my life. Does that make sense?"

I can barely speak for a moment, my knees feel so weak, I think I will just crumble right here onto the floor in front of him. No one has ever spoken so lovingly to me before, so tenderly, and with so much feeling in their voice. No one has ever cared this much. Until now. I am finally able to speak.

"Oh Ben, that makes beautiful, perfect sense to me, and yes, I am feeling the same way about you." He looks past me into the living room.

"Ah, I see exactly what I'm looking for."

I follow his gaze and smile when I see him headed for the tray of candles that I keep on my coffee table. As he lights them, I see where he is going with all of this, and decide to do my part too. I grab even more candles from the hall closet, and place them all around the living room. On top of the mantle, on the end tables, on top of the television. He follows behind me lighting each one. It's too warm to light the fireplace, but then I remember something. A DVD I had bought a few Christmases ago, before I bought this place and didn't have a real fireplace. I find it rather quickly and pop it into the DVD player.

Ben smiles widely, and leans down to kiss my neck.

"Ah, ah, ah. Not so fast. You want a perfect evening, you are going to get a perfect evening. Wait right here." He looks slightly puzzled as I give him a quick, soft kiss on his cheek, and head to my bedroom.

I am not a frilly girl, by any means. My sleeping attire is normally an old ratty t shirt, three sizes too big. That won't do tonight, and I know I have just the perfect thing, somewhere… There it is. A girl I went to the police academy with gave this to me for my birthday. I think she kind of meant it as a joke, but I thought it was pretty, and for some reason, just put it in the back of my closet. Where it has always stayed. Until now.

Ohhh, it's even prettier than I remembered. A long white satin and lace nightgown. It has very thin spaghetti straps and a very low, v front. It's cut down to my waist, and just lays softly on my breasts. Barely covering them, it's absolutely perfect.

I fluff my hair a little bit, it's especially wavy and curly tonight, which I know Ben likes. I stop and take one last look in the mirror. I have never given myself in this way to a man before. With so much feeling. Well, my old friend got the color of this gown right, I definitely feel like a virgin all over again.

I take a deep breath and head back to the living room. What a breathtaking sight. The whole living room is aglow in candlelight, a fire roaring on the TV, and there is Ben. He has spread the throw blanket from the back of the sofa onto the floor in front of the TV, and found every pillow I have, and put them on the blanket as well.

He takes my breath away. What an amazing sight. He has removed all of his clothing except for his boxers, and he's lying on the blanket, propped up on his elbow. What an incredible body he has. Rock hard abs, big, beefy arms, and the sexiest hip dents. Those lead right down to the biggest, thickest, cock I have ever seen. Of course, there is also that luxurious hair, those deep green eyes, and that captivating smile behind those soft, full lips.

But it's so much more than that. You only have to look at him, and you can actually see the warmth and tenderness emanate from him. That's my Ben. Yes, that's exactly how I think of him now, "My Ben".

The minute he sees me, he jumps to his feet. We slowly walk towards each other.

"Oh my God, Micki. You are the most incredibly beautiful woman, inside and out. You are amazing."

"Funny I was just thinking how very incredible and amazing you are as well." We wrap our arms around each other, and kiss softly. He tastes delicious.

"Micki, would you mind very much if I called you Michele? It just seems to suit you so much more, especially right now." I smile at that request.

"I would absolutely love it if you called me that. No one has used my full name for a very long time, and I love hearing you say it." It's so true, when he speaks my name, it is as if I have never heard my name said before. Like a choir of angels are singing it. He takes my hand in his and leads me to the blanket in front of the TV.

We sit down and he holds both of my hands. He has such a serious look on his face. Very thoughtful, like he is weighing every word so carefully before he even dares to speak.

"Michele, I want, no, I need, to say something to you. But I am so afraid that I'll ruin tonight by saying what I want to say." I squeeze his hand a little.

"It's okay Ben. Say whatever you need to say. Nothing will ruin tonight for us. I promise." I am really hoping that will be true, but he is starting to make me worry a little bit. What is he about to tell me that could ruin this perfect evening?

"Well, I can't look into your lovely face, and those beautiful eyes, hold you and touch you, and be so close to you anymore without saying this. So here goes." I smile at him, to let him know it is alright to continue, but I have to admit, I am getting very nervous as the seconds tick by.

He takes a deep breath and continues.

"Michele, I am falling so deeply and completely in love with you. I know this sounds crazy. Everything has happened so fast. I mean two days ago, we didn't even know each other and now I can't imagine my life without you. You may not feel the same way, and that's okay, but I just had to say it, I have to tell you how I feel, I am so afraid of scaring you away...

I place my finger on his lips, to quiet him.

"Oh Ben, I have tried to deny it, but I do feel the same way about you. It's so hard for me to say the words sometimes, but here goes. Yes, this is crazy, I know that we just met, but I am falling deeply and completely in love with you too."

The happiness we are feeling is very plain to see in our eyes and faces, we hug tightly and then kiss. Our kiss starts off so tender and sweet. But quickly turns deep and passionate. We fall back on the blanket, our lips still locked, and touch every single inch of each other. It is tender, and hot, and passionate, and loving, all at the same time.

I have never made love to a man that I was in love with before. It is much more intense, and real. So much meaning is involved. It is about so much more than just feeling pleasure. It is about giving myself, my heart and soul to this wonderful man.

This man that I love. That word is definitely getting easier to say now, to think, and to feel. We do make mad, passionate love that night, all through the night, just the way we wanted to. Slowly, so very slowly. We have explored every inch of each other's bodies with our lips, tongues, hands and fingers. Our clothes didn't even come off completely for the first hour. We have stayed completely intertwined, enraptured with each other. The ecstasy and pleasure are beyond words, the passion and love beyond belief.

When we catch our breath, we then start all over again, finding another position, a new way of saying I love you to each other.

It truly has been a perfect night, in every way, and I never want it to end.

Chapter Seven

As the sun starts to come up, we are laying quietly on our blanket, but not sleeping. We haven't slept all night. There was no time for that.

Our arms are wrapped around each other, our bodies intertwined, and we are giving each other, tender little kisses. On the nose, forehead, cheeks, eyelids…we just don't want to miss one tiny spot.

"I could stay like this forever, how about you?" I close my eyes, I would love nothing better, but now in the light of day, I don't know how long I do have. I can't count on forever anymore.

"Michele, what's wrong? Please talk to me.

This is about last night, in that alley, isn't it?"
That's the one problem with giving so much of
yourself to someone, it's so much harder to hide
the bad stuff from them.

"I'm sorry babe, I don't want to think about
that right now. This is our time, and it's perfect. I
only want to think about you, and us. I love you
Benjamin Brewer, and yes, I would love nothing
better than to stay just like this, with you,
forever!"

He gives me a huge smile, and I giggle, Yes, I
think for the first time in my life, I actually
giggle, and I feel euphoric, and filled with
happiness. With that, Ben holds me tightly as he
pulls me on top of him.

"Come here sexy, I'm not done with you yet."

He wraps his fingers in my hair and he kisses
me, wild and frenzied. Full of lightning and
thunder. There isn't going to be anything slow
about this time, we are both so ready for each
other, we want each other immediately.

I start on top. As I slide my wet opening
down onto his ready and willing cock, he cups
my breasts in his hands, kneading them and
tickling my diamond hard nipples. Then we roll
over and he's the one in control. He grabs a
handful of my hair and pulls my mouth as close
to his as we can physically get. Our tongues
fighting to get as far inside each other's mouths,

as they can. I grab his perfect ass cheeks, and dig in my fingernails. He lifts his head momentarily and bites his lower lip. With all of my might, I pound him as far and deep inside of me as I can get him. Our thrusts are intense and full, we grunt with each one. I can no longer breathe. As our orgasm fills the room, I stop breathing completely. We both cum from head to curling toes, and there is no room in our bodies for anything other than our earth shattering, thunderous, orgasms. Not even oxygen to take a breath with.

Once we have completely satisfied each other, and are drained of every ounce of our beings, we fall into each other's arms. Still shuddering, shaking and trembling, from the fiery orgasms we have just given each other.

We just can't seem to stop holding each other, we just don't seem to want to be apart for even one second. But, unfortunately, our perfect night is drawing to a close. I look at the clock on the TV, and realize that the morning has slipped through our fingers, and I will soon have to get up and face this day. Face my noon meeting at the station, which I am dreading more and more by the minute.

"You have to get up soon don't you?"

"I don't want to. But I guess I have to. I just don't want our time together to end."

"Oh, we'll have a whole lifetime of perfect nights, and days, and moments together. I promise you that, my love." I love hearing him say that, but can't believe it fully. Not with everything that I know might be headed for me.

"Oh, baby, you're shivering. Are you okay? You know that I'm not going to let anything happen to you, ever. I promise that on my life." Now I am really scared.

"No, don't say that. I'll be fine, but if anything ever happened to you because of me, I couldn't live with myself. You have to promise me that you'll take care of yourself, please be careful. Promise me?" The thought of anything happening to him is too much to bear.

"I promise. Now that I've found you, I'm not letting anything happen to either one of us. Everything is going to be okay, Michele. Do you believe me?"

"Oh yes, I do believe in you and trust you with my life. Even more importantly, I trust you with my heart and soul now too. In case you haven't noticed, I am all yours now, Ben. Every bit of me."

"I am going to take care of every bit of you. Always. I'm going to enjoy the hell out of it too!"

We smile and laugh, and kiss again. I will never get tired of kissing and touching this man.

There could never be any better feeling on this earth, than being in his arms.

I look at the clock again and there is no getting around it anymore, I have to get up. Then inspiration strikes…

"I know what will help get me motivated this morning, and into the shower…" I grab his hand and he smiles at me, knowing exactly what I mean, and we race into the bathroom. Laughing and giggling all the way, just like two carefree lovers, and that's exactly how I feel at this very moment. Free and so very alive.

The steam from the shower feels so good, of course Ben feels even better. It is undoubtedly the best shower I've ever had. We wash every inch of each other. With soapy fingers and hands, we caress and fondle our way to climax, yet again. We wrap ourselves up in a large bath sheet, and as I dry Ben's back, he gently dries my hair.

"Now that is the only way to take a shower!" I love the satisfaction and happiness in his voice.

"I agree completely, and wouldn't mind adding that to my daily routine."

"Consider it done, My Queen!" Ben said it jokingly, but my temper flares at hearing those words, and I fly into an immediate rage. I push him away, rather hard too, and scream at him.

"Don't EVER call me that, do you hear me?!

93

NEVER!"

"Whoa, whoa, what's wrong with you? What did I say? You mean the *my quee...*" I give him such a glare, he stops speaking immediately. I instantly feel so horrible, but those words, that phrase, brings a flood of horrible memories rushing back into my head. Memories that I have spent years trying to erase. I start to shake from head to toe, and then the tears come.

Ben rushes over to me, and hugs me so tightly, I can barely breathe.

"Oh my God, Michele, what's the matter baby? I am so, so sorry, I would never hurt you for anything in the world, I was only teasing. Look at me sweetheart, are you okay?" I am sobbing uncontrollably by now, and hug Ben just as tightly as he is holding me. I feel as if I am holding onto him for dear life, literally. I feel so awful for yelling at him like that, and so stupid too.

"Oh, Ben, I am so sorry. I didn't mean to scream at you like that. Just those words...they brought back some really bad memories. But I still didn't have any right to get so mad. Forgive me?" I have managed to stop crying, and look up into Ben's smiling face.

"Nothing to forgive, my love. I am just sorry about the bad memories, but all of that is going to change now. Now that we're together."

"I'm so sorry I ruined our perfect day."

"You didn't ruin anything. It was a perfect night, and it is a perfect day. Anytime we are together it's absolutely perfect, and it always will be. Are you feeling better now baby?"

"Yes, you always make me feel better. In fact whenever you're near me, I feel incredibly wonderful!"

"Good, that's how it should be. Now let me kiss away those tears."

Ben kisses every last teardrop that had managed to escape from my eyes, and I have to make sure that the morning really does end perfectly, so I kiss his lips, and make sure he knows how I want to make things truly right again.

Chapter Eight

When we finally manage to get dressed, after making love one last time. I know it's time for me to leave. I feel like a condemned woman walking to the gallows as Ben and I walk to our cars, arm in arm, naturally!

"Do you want me to go to the station with you baby? I can tell this meeting has you upset. If you need to talk about it, I'm here."

"I know, and I'm fine. Just police stuff, that's all. Knowing I'll be seeing you tonight, will get me through it."

"I'll be at the station early tonight, so we can grab some alone time, maybe before your shift starts?"

"Sounds perfect to me. Now don't you have a job to do too?"

"Yeah, I guess I need to at least put in an appearance at the paper today."

"You must be tired honey, you didn't get any sleep last night, try to get a nap in today."

"Nah, don't need one, I am wide awake. I feel completely exhilarated."

"Gee, so do I." We squeeze each other and kiss one last time.

"Michele, promise me that you'll be careful!"

"I will, I promise. I love you Ben." I take myself by complete surprise. I have never said those words to anyone before. But the look on Ben's face, makes me very glad that I have said them now.

"Oh Michele, I love you too. Now get going sexy. I'll follow you to the station and then head over to the paper." I roll my eyes, and smile at him.

"Now, none of that. I told you I'm taking care of you now, so get used to it." He winks at me, and grins with that brilliant, gleaming smile of his. Oh how I do love this man. Me, Michele Maureen Murphy, head over heels, totally and completely, so in love, with the most wonderful man on earth! Me, the tough girl, police officer. I never would've believed it could be possible, but here I am, and here he is, and I've never been happier in my entire life!

Love, love, love. I even love saying the word!

97

I feel like I'm walking on air. I've always thought people who talked about love like this were so corny and simple. But who knew, they were right all along. All of the songs I've sang along to all of my life, all of the romance novels I've loved reading, the poems and sonnets too…they are all true after all! I am so happy to have found that out, before it was too late.

When I get to the station house door, I turn to wave to Ben, but he is already gone. That's odd, I know he would've waited to make sure I was safely inside. I'm sure traffic probably got in the way. Okay, off to the gas chamber.

I have to stop in the locker room to ready myself for this meeting. I want to put my uniform on, and pull my hair into a tight ponytail. This has nothing to do with *them*, but it helps me get into the attitude I will need in that room. I can't be myself around them, relaxed and carefree. I never could. I have to be strong and tough, and ready for anything.

I take a deep breath and leave the locker room. As soon as I open the door, I see Jack standing there waiting for me.

"Hey Micki, how are you holding up?"

"I just want to get this over with. I'll be fine."

"Are you sure you want to go through with this?"

"I would give anything not to, but we both

know that I have to. So let's just get it done."

"I'll be right by your side kid."

"Thanks Jack" I appreciate my partner's fatherly role during this, and give him a little hug to show him that.

As we walk into the waiting room of Lt. Dorcett, I am shocked to see Olga sitting at the receptionist's desk. She is ancient, I can't believe she hasn't retired by now.

"Hi Olga, I have an appointment with the Lieutenant."

"Let me announce you dear." Olga picks up the phone on her desk, she is moving in slow motion. Really time for her to retire.

After what seemed like ten minutes, she finally buzzed the line on the other side of that door.

"Officer Murphy and her partner, Officer Dunbar are here sir. Uh huh, okay. I'll tell her."

"You can go in now dear, but only you. Officer Dunbar will have to wait here." Jack is not happy about that bit of news.

"Hey, now wait a minute, that wasn't part of the deal." Jack is getting upset very quickly, and heading for the door. Olga attempts to get up from behind her desk, but that is really pointless, since she can barely straighten up. I grab Jack's arm before he can go any further.

"Jack, Jack. It's okay. Let me go in alone, I'll

be okay. Just let me do this, get it over and done with."

"No, Micki, I should be in there with you. You might need me."

"If I do, believe me you'll know. It'll be alright. Just sit down and wait for me, it won't take long."

"Damn it, Micki, this doesn't feel right. It's not sitting right in my gut."

"I know, I am feeling the same way, but it'll be okay. It has to be now."

"Okay, okay, but if they try anything, or you need me, I am right outside this door, and so help me God, I'll bust in there if I have to and take them all on."

"I know Jack, just stay calm. I'll be right out." I give Jack a little "I'll be okay" smile, pat him on the arm, and walk into the "chamber of hell", at least that's how I'd always thought of it.

"Well, hello Officer Murphy, so nice to see you again."

"Hello, Uncle Anthony."

"I'm very happy we are not being so formal this afternoon, Michaelina." Oh how I bristle at that name. I can actually feel a snarl come up out of my throat.

"I see you still have a problem with your given name. You cannot expect me to call you by that hideous name you chose for yourself,

Michele, wasn't it?" I glare at him, no he cannot call me by that name. That name is reserved for someone so far superior to this man, this creature, sitting across the room from me. I only want to hear that name come from the lips of one man, from now on, and forever.

"No, I wouldn't expect that at all, call me anything you like."

"I was hoping you would've come in here with a better attitude than this, Michaelina. It's been so long since we've seen each other, and we are family after all."

"I honestly don't think of us as family. All of you made that very clear to me many years ago."

"Ah, my dear, lets' not dredge up ancient history. We will never agree on why you felt the need to abandon your family, maybe we should discuss more urgent matters instead."

"That's why I'm here. He's back, isn't he?"

"Yes, my child, he is. Surely you were not naïve enough to believe that he had actually been killed the last time. I had assumed that of all people, you would surely know the truth?"

"Of course I knew he was still alive, but I thought I had your assurance of protection. Why didn't you tell me that he had come back here?"

"We didn't feel it was necessary that you be privy to that knowledge. We will take care of him, when and if the time comes."

"What do you mean, it wasn't necessary?? He tortured and killed my parents, he tried to rape and kidnap me! How can it NOT be necessary to tell me that he's back??"

"Those were all unfortunate events, of course, but still, you had a lot to do with those decisions. Things could have gone quite differently, had you chosen differently, and you know it, Michaelina."

"I cannot believe that you would blame me for any part of that! How dare you insinuate that I had anything to do with the death of my parents, all because I wouldn't marry that possessed madman! I'm beginning to think you are as mad as he is!"

"Please, please, calm down, my dear. We will achieve nothing from this meeting, with you screaming and wailing already. Please sit down, we have much to discuss."

I know better than to fly off the handle so soon. Uncle Anthony is a man who demands respect, whether he deserves it or not. I have to calm down, if I want any answers, and his help in killing Heinrick for the last time.

I slowly sit down in the chair across the desk from him. As I get closer, I can tell that Anthony is rather enjoying this, the feeling of having control over me. I hate him for that, and I always have.

"Now that's better. You have many questions, what would you like to ask me?"

"Why haven't you stopped him yet? Those women he killed, especially the last one. We both know they were calling cards for me. To try to get my attention. Those women died for no reason other than his vengeance against me. How can you let that happen?" I was pleading with him now, not just out of my own fear, but for the women he's killed and all of the ones he will kill if he isn't stopped.

"He may have been trying to get your attention, and ours as well, but mostly they were just a food source. There's nothing wrong with that, really." I can feel the rage rising in me, I can't believe what I'm hearing.

"Please tell me that you are not serious about that?! You can't really feel that way. That is monstrous!"

"Michaelina, you have completely forgotten where you come from, our ways. How sad, I didn't realize how "*human*" you'd become. I do believe that even your parents would be disappointed by you, well your father at least."

I can no longer contain my anger, and it pulls me up out of my seat. My voice rises, and I place my hands on his desk, and lean forward. I don't want him to miss one word. I want to look close in his eyes, so he can see my hatred for him.

"Don't you ever mention my parents to me, they both hated you and your ways just as much as I do, maybe even more. Why do you think they raised me in the human world, away from the entire family?"

"My dear child, I will tell you exactly what I told them the day they left the clan. You cannot change what and who you are. Never. It will follow you for all of eternity, you cannot escape your heritage, and you should be honored by it, not turn your back on it. You foolish little girl! They would still be alive today had they just turned you over to Heinrick, and the world would lay at your feet. Instead you turned your back on us, your family, and your parents paid with their lives. So tell me now, my dear, was it worth it?"

I can feel tears burning my eyes, but I refuse to give in to them, I will not give him the pleasure of knowing that he is getting to me.

"My parents were slaughtered by an insane madman, trying to protect me. All they ever wanted was for me to have a normal life, and they died trying to give me exactly that. I honor them, I will never honor you and what you are."

He throws his head back, his laughter filling the room. It chills me to the bone. Then as he slowly brings his head back, he looks me in the eye, and I am sickened. The fluorescent lights are gleaming off of his fangs.

"You sick bastard! There's nothing funny about this. Too many people have died and are dying still at his hands. What are you going to do about him?" I am screaming at him now, and a back door opens and two of my very large cousins come gliding into the room.

"Is everything alright, Father?"

"Yes, yes, my sons. Say hello to your cousin Michaelina."

They just glare at me. Their fangs had come out the minute they entered the room, feeling the agitation in the air.

"Hello Jonathan. Hello Matthias." I speak to them in a tone completely void of any emotion. They snarl at me, and refuse to speak.

"Now, now boys. Don't be like that. Michaelina was just stating her feelings. We must remember that she has been removed from our ways and our family for many years now. She is not fully to blame for her behavior."

Chapter Nine

My cousins go and stand behind their father, one on either side of him. They are showing me in their own subtle way that I need to tone it down. I know that I need to try to calm down a little at least. My rage will get nothing accomplished with my uncle, and if I get any louder, Jack might come storming through that door. That would get ugly, very quickly. I sit back down in my seat, and try to relax before I speak again.

"Uncle Anthony, you know that no one else can handle this. You, all of you in the task force, are the only ones who can destroy him for good."

"Destroy him? Why would we want to destroy him?" He seems totally amazed that I would even suggest such a thing.

"I know that you don't care about my life anymore, but he is killing innocent people. We all know he won't stop this time. So he must be stopped, you must end this." If I hadn't known better, I would've thought I saw a glimpse of hurt in my uncle's eyes.

"I can assure you that he is being closely watched, if he threatens to make our world known to the humans in any way, we will take care of him. We would take the necessary steps to make sure he would not be able to ruin everything that we have worked centuries to maintain."

"I don't understand, you have him under surveillance, why not just take him out permanently? Stake and decapitate him, don't let any more innocents die."

"Oh my naïve, misguided girl. Don't you understand, he is one of us. He may not be worthy of our loyalty, but we feel for him exactly what you feel for those dead women. Pity."

"So you refuse to help?"

"As I have stated, we are watching him. If he strays too far and endangers us with his existence, we will do what we must."

I feel so frustrated, and angry, and yes, scared. I don't know if I can stop him, but it's very clear that I am on my own in this. I don't know how it will end, but I know the outcome should be clear very soon. Heinrick has made that very evident with his last victim.

"Well, I guess this meeting is over., there's nothing more to say." I stand up to head for the door.

"Don't leave so soon, my child. We are just getting reacquainted. It's been such a pleasure seeing you again."

"I wish I could say the same. I was expecting, hoping, for a different outcome, I guess."

"I'm sorry you are disappointed. Things are the way they are meant to be. There is something you need to remember. You are vampire, whether you want to be or not. If the need arises you can take care of yourself. You need to allow it through, though. You must allow it out." Well that thought is making me sick to my stomach.

"Yeah, okay, I'll remember that. Thanks." I can feel the bile coming up into my throat. I hope he can hear the sarcasm dripping in my words. I have my hand on the door knob, I will be so relieved to get out of here, to be on the other side of this door.

"Oh, Michaelina, one last thing." Damn! So close to getting out of here. I turn my head and look at him, but keep a firm hand on the knob. That doorknob feels like security gripped in my hand.

"You can, and will take care of yourself when the time arises, just as I said. But your new *friend*, Benjamin Brewer, isn't that his name? Well, he may not possess the same capabilities that you do my dear."

Oh no, Oh no, my Ben! My heart starts to race, and my eyes fill with tears. If he was hoping to get a reaction from me, he is getting a very strong one now.

"How do…what do you…if you EVER harm him in any way, shape, or form…I swear to you on my life, on the lives of every member of your family, I will destroy you, and take great pleasure in doing so. Do you understand me?!"

I don't think I have ever spoken with so much anger and vile hatred before, if I still had my fangs they would be completely extended, and thirsty for his life.

"Ah, now, now, Michaelina. See, my sons, I told you it was true." I am still so livid, I am barely comprehending what he is saying.

"What the hell are you talking about? I meant every word I just said."

"I know you do, and that makes me so very proud, my dear. You are more vampire than you realize. I just proved it to you."

I say nothing more, I just glare at my uncle, and run out the door. I growl as I slam the door behind me. Olga and Jack look at me immediately, startled. Jack hurries over to me. I grab his arm, and we get the hell out of that office. I can't stop for anything, I have to get to Ben.

"Micki, Micki, slow down. What happened in there?"

"I have to see Ben. He's not safe."

"Is that what he told you in there? What else did he say?"

"A lot of shit. Mostly that I'm on my own in this."

"Oh no you're not. **We** are in this together." That stops me dead in my tracks.

"No Jack! I will not have anything happen to you! You are the closest thing I have to a father. I will not allow you to get involved in this! Do you hear me?"

"I hear you loud and clear, but that doesn't change a damn thing. You are not doing this alone. You're like a daughter to me Micki, I'll never let any harm come to you. Ever! Do you hear me?"

"Okay, okay "*Dad*". I hear you loud and clear. I need to go splash some water on my face, compose myself a little bit. Please wait here for me."

"Yeah, take a few minutes, and clear your head. We both need to be on our top game now, and plan our next move."

"You've never said anything truer, Jack. I'll be right out."

I head into the locker room, but turn to look back at Jack.

"Hey Jack. Thanks. I love you." No time like the present to make sure the people I love know it. I dash inside before he can respond. Anything he'd say would just make me cry right now. I have to stay calm, and focus. I take out my cell and call Ben.

"C'mon, babe, please pick up. Please, please answer your phone." Five rings, damn, where is he? His voice mail picks up.

"Hi babe. Please call me as soon as you get this message. Just need to hear your voice. Okay, I'll talk to you later then. Oh, Ben, I love you."

It was hard not to sound choked up when I spoke, when all I want to do is scream and cry. But that won't help anything right now. I need to see him, just to know that he's safe. Once I know he's okay, then I can concentrate on finding Heinrick. Not a happy thought, but I know it has to be done.

I pull a bench over to the window, climb up, and jump out. I have to get out of here before Jack gets suspicious. I will not let Jack kill himself by trying to protect me. I refuse to lose any more people that I love.

I land in the brick alley below and head for

the parking lot. I try reaching Ben again on the way to my car. Still no answer. I'll go to the paper, that's where he was headed. Maybe he doesn't get good cell reception in the building. He's probably sitting at his desk right now, working on his story. How I hope that's exactly where he is. He'll see me, wrap his strong arms around me and we'll kiss passionately. We are always so hungry for each other, I know that will never go away.

I can't believe all of this damn traffic, it's going to take forever to get there. If anything happens to Ben, I'll never forgive myself, or my "family". I never think of them as that, but Uncle Anthony is right, there is no escaping it.

There is also no escaping, no matter how hard I try, what I really am. I have spent my lifetime, running away from it. I've done everything I can to be as human as I can be. I've denied my true self, and I don't regret it. My parents died so that I could live my life, the way I always wanted to, free.

Most of us don't live the old lifestyle anymore. Only some of the ancient ones like Uncle Anthony and his clan still do. They enjoy the prestige and power too much to ever give it up. Us "Newstyles" as we call ourselves, take great pains to eradicate every part of the vampire world from our lives. Even going to the great length of having our fangs filed and capped every three months or so. They constantly rejuvenate and grow, so that has to be done. Otherwise we have no control over when they extend. I have squelched every extra sense that I was "born" with. I have turned my back on my entire heritage, just to be something I'm not…human.

Isn't it funny that now, the very thing I turned my back on, might be the only thing that saves my life, and the lives of the people I love. It's always there though, what I am. I feel it, and it's a constant struggle to push it away. Especially this week, when I met Ben. I had always heard of the **Blitztreach**, a word and legend handed down for thousands upon thousands of years from our German and Celtic ancestors. But I never thought it was real. It was always told to me that when a vampire meets their one true life mate, they experience an overpowering, undeniable, desire and yearning and hunger for that person. It's said that the longing never goes away, and that the sex is incredible between the vampire and their eternal mate. There is no denying that is exactly how I feel with Ben. It's very rare for it to happen between a vampire and human though. But there is no other explanation.

Just being near to him that first time, it was

like an electrical storm in my whole body. Every time I touch him, every kiss, every, everything, I must have him. Our bodies long to be one, even just the scent of him makes me drunk with ecstasy and passion for him.

Believe me, if I did have my fangs, they would've come out every time I was with him. I wanted to bite him so badly every time we made love. I wanted to drink from him, and share my blood with him as well. I've never experienced this feeling of such ultimate desire before, and I know with my entire being that I never will again. Not for anybody but Ben. He is my life mate, the one I am meant to be with for eternity. I remember my mother and father teaching me about blitztreach. But that was in happier times. It is nice to know now though that they did feel this for each other, even when they were divided over the newstyle life. They still felt this, right up until the end.

I may have turned my back on the vampire life, and have never really cared about being immortal before. I've never really given it much thought, but now I have something to live that long for. My time with Ben. I never had to worry before about wanting to tell anyone what I am. Jack knows, he found out the last time Heinrick was around. The task force had to step in. There was a huge cover up, and Jack had to be told. He was too smart of a cop, he would've figured most of it out eventually, anyway.

The human police thought they had killed Heinrick, they thought he was just a drug crazed, psychopath. But Uncle Anthony and his family had to step in. But they had only maimed him. That was seven years ago, it has taken him that long to recover. Not long enough, as far as I am concerned. If only they had killed him, no one else would be suffering right now.

Vampires, as a race, are as varied as humans. Depending on when they were turned, and which family, or clan, as we call them, turned them. Vampires have progressed so much through the years, or should I say centuries. Thanks to all of the scientific and medical breakthroughs some of our race have developed. But different clans follow different guidelines, and have different beliefs. I come from a very advanced clan. We are day walkers, and no longer need to feed on humans for our existence. Uncle Anthony's side of the family has also progressed, but they cling to the older belief system. They feel so superior to humans, and only adhere to the more modern ways out of necessity, so they can mainstream more easily.

But there are still clans that have never progressed at all. They want to stay as true to the original ways as they can. They sleep during daylight, it can't even touch their skin, and they kill humans to feed, but mostly just for fun. That is the style of clan that Heinrick comes from. Those families are exactly why Uncle Anthony's special task force was created, to keep the "Ancients" in line. Human police officers would never stand a chance against those ones.

Chapter Ten

Thankfully, I'm finally here! Oh, please, please let Ben be here, please.

"Hello, may I help you Officer?" The receptionist sees me before I notice her. This place is huge.

"Yes, you can. I need to see Ben Brewer. It's rather important."

"I'll be happy to call Mr. Brewer for you." She picks up her phone and dials. It seems like it is taking forever for her to talk. Finally she gets an answer.

"Hello, yes. There's a police officer here…" She covers the mouthpiece with her hand. "I'm sorry miss, can I tell him what you're here in reference to?" My heart is leaping, oh I am so thankful he's here and okay. Any moment now,

I'll be in his arms again.

"It's, just tell him it's Michele."

"She says her name is Michele. Yes sir. Okay sir." She hangs up the phone. I bet he's on his way to the lobby right now. I can hardly contain my excitement and relief.

"That was the editor miss, he hasn't seen Mr. Brewer since yesterday." My heart drops all the way to the floor. I feel panicked.

"Is he absolutely sure? Has he heard from him at all? This is very important."

"I can call him back again, if you like." She seems like she is getting a little annoyed with me, but I don't care, I have to find Ben.

"Yes, please. I wouldn't bother you if it wasn't vitally important."

She picks up the phone again and this time she must have dialed the editor directly, because he has taken the call right away.

"Hello sir. The officer is still here, the one inquiring about Mr. Brewer. Yes, she'd like to know if you've been in contact with Mr. Brewer at all."

"Tell him I'm one of the officers Ben is doing the ride along with." I thought he might be more forthcoming with answers if he knew who I was, and not just some groupie or crazed cop looking for Ben.

"She says she's one of the police officers that

Mr. Brewer has been doing the ride along with, yes that's right. Uh huh, uh huh. Okay, yes, I will tell her sir." She hangs up and speaks quickly. I think she's worried that I'll have her call again and ask even more questions.

"He said to tell you that the last time he saw Mr. Brewer was yesterday afternoon in the research department. He hasn't talked to him since."

"Okay, thank you. If you see Ben, I mean, Mr. Brewer, could you please tell him to call Michele immediately. It's very important."

"Yes, miss. I will tell him, and I'll leave a note for him on his desk too in case I don't happen to be here when he comes in."

"Thank you."

Oh shit. What now? I have to calm down and think. Maybe he went home. I'll try his apartment. Damn it, I don't know where he lives. If I could just tap into my extra senses, I would be able to tell. But that will take too long, I'm too out of practice. It'll be faster to call the station and just get his address from his ride along form.

Patty looks up the information for me, and also tells me that Jack is looking for me, and is furious. Oh well, he'll have to get over that. I just hope he goes home to Betty and doesn't get any more involved in this. It would kill me if

119

anything happened to him because of me.

Good, I'm almost there. Think good thoughts Michele, and he'll be there. Working on his story on his laptop, or taking that much needed nap, that I asked him to take. I take a deep breath, and ring the doorbell. Nothing. I ring it again, and again. I lean on it, still nothing. Maybe he can't hear the bell, or it's not working. I pound on the door with my fist. He'd definitely hear that, even if he's sleeping. Well, it's painfully obvious that he's not here. One last place to look, my place. If he's not there, I need to face facts, even if they scare me to death.

I drive like a maniac, I get to my house in sixteen minutes flat. I definitely just broke some laws, lots of them. But I don't care, nothing matters now except Ben.

He's not outside, and his car isn't anywhere around. He can't get inside, but maybe he left a phone message. I run inside, and straight to the phone. Nothing. Okay I can't deny it any longer, something is horribly wrong. I have a feeling, a very strong one that I know where I'll find him, and it's my worst possible nightmare.

I only have a few hours of daylight left, I have to find Heinrick before nightfall. It'll be best to get to him while he's still in his coffin, or whatever he's using for a bed this time. With every instinct I have, I now know that if I find

Heinrick, I'll find Ben.

I must think, where could he be? I have to think this through. He's a creature of habit. Old habits. The most logical place would be the manor where his family lived for hundreds of years, but that house was condemned and torn down long ago. That whole section of the city was rezoned for businesses and warehouses. A warehouse in that area might be comfortable for him, it's on the waterfront and the water is very attractive to vampires. It actually enhances our powers.

Water is full of energy, and it allows us to be stronger. I may have abandoned the vampire ways, but certain physical aspects are simply impossible to escape. I must admit I do like the extra strength the water gives me, especially when we happen to find ourselves on the waterfront, trying to apprehend someone. I enjoy the look on Jack's face when that happens. A little pride, definitely chagrin, and even a tiny bit of envy too, I think. Jack is all human, but he would really enjoy some of the benefits of being vampire.

Okay, I need to get down there. I grab my map and go. I don't know if I'm going to remember where the site of Heinrick's house was. So many things change in that area constantly. If I could just concentrate for a minute, maybe I could hone in on the right spot. But I can't think about anything but Ben at this moment. If anything happens to him, I just can't bear the thought of life without him now. He has to be alright. I have to make sure that he's alright.

He has to live so I can tell him the truth about me. No more secrets between us ever. I've never been faced with having to tell someone what I truly am, but then again, I've never been in love before either. But I will tell Ben the truth, even if it means losing him. Eventually, he will notice that I'm not aging. When we are turned as a child, we stop aging at a certain point in adulthood. He'll see the daily shots I have to give myself to live an almost completely human life, and the fact that I won't be dying of natural causes.

I refuse to lie to Ben anymore. If we both get out of this safely, I just have to make sure we get out of this safely. I'll be honest with him always. All I ever want to do is love him and be with him for the rest of his life, if he'll have me. Now I just have to find him.

Oh crap, all these buildings look so different since the last time I was down here. My GPS won't even help, I don't remember the exact address. I have to be able to do this. To use my vampire skills. I just have to close my eyes, concentrate, relax and take a deep breath. It's so difficult. It's been too long…damn it!

"If the need arises you can take care of yourself. You need to allow it through, though. You must allow it out." The words of Uncle Anthony are so loud in my head. It's all I can hear right now. Okay all I have to do is relax, concentrate and "let it through". Just *let it through*…that's it, that's it, right there! Mulligan Plastics. I know Heinrick is in there, I can sense him, and I can smell Ben. His scent is as sweet as candy to me. I smell blood too, oh no, he's hurt.

I don't have much daylight left, I have to get in there right now, and get him out of there…before Heinrick wakes up for his next feeding. I have to be quick, but very quiet. Shit, the door is padlocked shut. I can't shoot it off, too much noise. I have to look for another way in. Maybe a window. There should be some in the alley behind the factory. That would be a better place to go in anyway. I am no longer thinking about my next step, I am following my instincts. Not my police instincts, but another, even stronger sense. It just seems to be pulling me in a certain direction, and I would be stupid not to listen to it.

Just as I thought, there are a bunch of windows in the alley. Now just to find the right one. I need to slow down, breathe deeply, and just go where it takes me. Stop, that one right there in the middle. Damn, I am too short to reach it. It really sucks being this short sometimes. Not one box, crate, or anything else, anywhere that I can see in this whole damn alley to climb up on. I wonder…..hmmmmm.

I used to be so good at jumping years and years ago. Maybe I am hoping for too much to get all of my abilities back at once…but I am losing too much time just standing here. So I'll try it, the worst that can happen is I fall. I need to get in there now, I need to get to Ben before it's too late!

One, two, three…*whoooosh*…holy shit, I did it. I am at the window, crouched on the sill. The frame is all rotted wood, I should be able to push it in easily. *Creeeekkkk…thunk*…okay, it's open. It's not too far of a jump down, I just have to do it quietly. *Phuummp*…oh Ben, please be okay. I'm coming.

My gun drawn, I start slowly moving behind high stacks of old, dusty boxes. It looks like there's some light towards the center of the warehouse. I just need to get around this last row of boxes….oh my dear God…no, it can't possibly be…that can't possibly be Ben…

I have tunnel vision immediately, all I can see is the horrific scene before my eyes. As I step closer, my eyes widen at the horror. There in the very center of the warehouse is my beloved Ben. He's chained to a wooden beam more than fifteen feet off of the ground. His head is hanging down, he looks all beaten and bloodied. I can see from here that his body looks limp and lifeless. He's so pale, so motionless. He looks *dea*...no, I can't even think the word. It can't be. I won't let it be!

I am almost at the beam...looking up I can see him more clearly. He's so bruised and there's blood dripping out of the side of his mouth, and blood all over his clothing. Oh my love, what has he done to you?

In my softest voice, barely above a whisper, I have to get him to open his eyes.

"Ben, Ben sweetheart. It's me, Michele. I'm here, can you hear me? I'm going to get you out of here. Can you open your eyes? Oh Ben please, please open your eyes for me."

What the...? "Let me go, let me go." So quickly, huge hands are wrapped around my arms, holding me so tightly, I can't move an inch. Two very large men are holding me firm. I kick them, as hard as I can. First the one on the left, then the goon on my right. Neither one of them is even phased at my attempt of violence.

Oh no, my worst fear realized...I can smell *him*. He must be very close.

"Hello my lovely Michaelina. Oh how I have

waited for this moment." If I wasn't being held so firmly in this spot, I would've jumped ten feet in the air, he's right behind me. I can feel, and smell, his disgusting breath on my neck.

"Heinrick. It's you." I don't understand, it's not quite sundown yet, how can he be awake?

"Oh there's quite a simple explanation for that my lovely." Shit, I forgot, he can hear my thoughts, I have to be careful what I think. His vile laughter echoes in the huge warehouse.

"I see you haven't lost your sense of humor dear one. You can try to hide your thoughts, but I can tell what you're feeling too. So you needn't bother expending any extra energy on such silliness."

"So are you going to answer my question or not then?"

"But of course. I am actually proud to do so. Just as your clans have had many breakthroughs, we have also had some breakthroughs of our own. Most of them we have stolen from your kind, and just modified them to suit our needs. I was happy to give myself that little shot today that you use to allow you in the sunlight. I have been waiting for this day for such a long time."

He slowly runs his cold, dead fingers through my hair. Loosening it, and brushing it away from my neck. He bends down, and inhales the scent of my neck deeply. Then rests his hand on my shoulder. His touch makes me wince.

"Oh don't be that way Michaelina. After all, you are mine."

"I will never be yours, you sick, sadistic, bastard! Don't touch me." I scream at him.
A small, broken voice interrupts. "Michele…"
I look up and see Bens' eyes barely open. He starts coughing, and I can see him grimace in pain.

"Ben! I'm here sweetheart. Please don't try to talk, don't try to move. I will get you out of here."

"Leave her alone. Just kill me and let her go."
He can barely get the words out. There is more blood coming from his mouth. I don't think he can last much longer. I have to do something.

"I knew you'd be back someday. So okay, you win. Now let him go. You have what you came here for, me. Just let him go, and I'll do whatever you want."

"Ah, If only it were that simple dearest. I am almost done with him though, and then I'll get started with you." All I can do is close my eyes, I don't want to face this nightmare.

Heinrick slowly, purposefully, walks around me, so that he can speak to my face.

"Ahhh, you are every bit as beautiful as I remember. So indescribably beautiful. I have dreamed of this very moment so many times. To

127

look at your stunning face, feel your soft skin beneath my touch. Now to gaze into those radiant green eyes of yours. Michaelina, open your eyes please." I just can't do it, I don't want to look at him.

"Maybe you need a little assistance?"

His goons are squeezing my arms so tightly, it feels like they are being ripped off at the elbows.

"OWWWW."

"God damn you, leave her alone." My eyes fly open to see Ben struggling against the chains, he is using every last bit of strength that he has to try to free himself. But it is useless. He is bound too tightly, his body too weak. I can see how much agony he is in.

"Ben, Ben…listen to me. Stop moving. I am okay, I swear I am alright. I'm not hurt, just please stay as still as you can. We are going to be fine, I promise."

"Don't lie to the poor boy Michaelina. Let him enjoy his last few minutes on earth. Well, let them be honest at least." I turn to face him, and he is even more atrociously ugly than I remember. His skin is so blindingly white, his eyes sunken in with dark circles under them. His cheek bones jut out so far that his face hollows beneath them. He is so tall and bony, it's impossible to believe that he ever could've been alive at one time. That he was an actual human being…there is no trace of one left anywhere in him.

"Why are you doing this to him? He's not the one you came for."

"No, of course he isn't, but sometimes even the most detailed and thought out plans need to be altered. Imagine my disappointment, when I came back to collect what was due me…only to find out that you had found your life mate. So suddenly too, and after I had gone to so much trouble to leave all of those little love notes for you."

The thought of him referring to all of those innocent women that he had killed as "love notes" enrages me and I spit right in his face.

"How dare you talk about those women like that. You killed them for no reason at all, just to satisfy your own selfish needs. You sick, twisted, disgusting, mother fucker." He wipes the spittle from his face with his bony, claw like, finger.

"Such an awful way to talk to your future husband, My Queen."

I look up at Ben, and see his eyes widen, and I know that the realization of why that phrase had bothered me so has just hit him. He closes his eyes and winces at the pain of it.

"I will never be your queen, you son of a bitch. I loathe you, I despise everything you are. I would rather die than be tied to you in any way."

"I was so hoping that you would have a better attitude about all of this my lovely. But I think you will come around...you really have no other choice. In case you are forgetting, I have a little insurance hanging right above you."

Chapter Eleven

"You see my dear, your life mate is here to insure that you go through with your nuptials. He is going to be my best man, so to speak. Just wait until you see the delightful things I have in store for him, if you choose not to acquiesce." He actually seems excited at the thought of torturing Ben even more.

"In case you've forgotten, you were betrothed to me even before you were turned. You do indeed belong to me, and you will be my wife tonight. You will be mine in every way."

He steps closer to me and places his hand on my thigh, moving it further inside and then up higher and higher, until his fingers are brushing against me. I try to keep my legs closed, and push his hand away with my hips, but he is just too strong. His age has only made him stronger, and he easily pushes my thighs open with one finger. He rips my pants away with one swipe of his long, razor sharp, fingernails.

I have to turn away, I can't bear to look at this "thing" that's touching me, and I can't bear to look at Ben, knowing what he is watching.

"Get your hands off of her, I'll kill you, you ugly son of a bitch." He sounds so desperate, and he's getting weaker by the minute.

Thankfully Heinrick only strokes me a couple of times and then steps back. His excitement is plain to see.

"Mmm…I must be patient. I want everything to be perfect. I even have your gown ready and waiting for you." He starts to glide away, this could be my chance. But he suddenly stops in his tracks, turns around and looks at me.

"So you are still looking for a way to get out of here and save that pitiful excuse for a man? I guess my words aren't enough for you, you need an example of my promises."

He nods to a shadowy figure that I hadn't noticed before on a wooden plank near the beam that Ben is affixed to. I hadn't seen that plank before. It was hidden by the setting sun, and the shadows in this room. The figure that Heinrick has nodded to, is even larger than the two vampires who are holding me. He has something in his hand, I can't quite make out what it is.

There's something shiny that the overhead lights are glinting off of, it's long and thin.

He's starting to move now, he must be getting some kind of silent order from his master. He's walking towards Ben. I look at Heinrick, there's a look of pure excitement on his face, a look of absolute pleasure. I look back up at the vampire, and he's coming out of the shadows, I can now see better. I look directly at what he's holding, and no, oh no…it's a handsaw. I am struggling and straining to get loose, but the grip on my arms only tightens.

The vampire is next to Ben now, holding the saw at his wrist.

"Noooooooo, Heinrick, no please. I am begging you, don't do this, I'll do whatever you want. I'll marry you tonight. Just please don't hurt him anymore." Tears are uncontrollably running down my face. I am sobbing and pleading for the life of the only man I'll ever love.

"Now, now my Queen. I am thrilled at your change of heart, but I still think you need a tiny demonstration of what will happen if you should change your mind back the other way again."

The torturer takes the saw and starts to cut Ben's wrist. With all of the strength that Ben has left in his broken body, he lets out a blood curdling scream, and then goes limp. Either from loss of consciousness, or he is dead.

"NOOOOOOOOOOOOOO, BEN, NOOOOOOOO, OH PLEASE NO…" I am completely hysterical, I can't think, I am numb all over. My head starts spinning, the whole room is spinning. It's getter darker, and darker. I feel like I'm moving backwards and the room is getting smaller and smaller.

I'm awake now, my face is still so wet from my tears. I am still sobbing slightly. I open my eyes and look up, I need to see him, see if it's really true. He's not there, his body is not there. I start to panic. What did they do with him? Where did they take his body? I move my head to look around the room…but this isn't the warehouse. How did I get here?

I am no longer in that filthy room filled with dusty and dirty boxes. I am back in my childhood home. I am in the house where I was "born", where I lived so many wonderful and happy years with my parents.

I don't understand, how can this be? I must be hallucinating. This just isn't possible. But yet, here I am, in the main entryway. The same baroque wallpaper that Mother loved and Father hated so much. The plush carpeting that I used to love running barefoot on, just for the feel of it. This is all so crazy. I must've snapped and gone completely insane when I saw Ben get killed. That's the only explanation.

I hear voices coming from the formal living room. I head for the door, and as I do, I pass by the large mirror in the foyer and see my reflection. No, this can't be happening, I am in a long, black silk gown. I've worn this gown before, no I can't go through this again.

The voices are getting louder, there's a loud scream…I run to the door and quickly open it, unable to stop myself. I know what's behind that door, it's my nightmare personified. I don't want to face this again, I can't. But it's too late I am in the room now. No, no, no. I start shaking my head, and I cover my mouth to stifle my cries. I immediately see my parents. My mother and father both chained to large columns near the entrance to the dining room.

The scream had come from my mother. There's a huge man, he must be almost seven feet tall, and he's pouring drops of molten silver on her. It's burning her so badly. She is screaming in agony. My father is straining to get free, but can't. He is screaming obscenities at the disfigured man seated in the chair to the left of me…Heinrick.

"MOTHER! Stop hurting her right now! Do you hear me?!" Strong arms are binding me.

"It's…it's…okay…my darling. I'll be alright."

My mother could barely speak. She could barely breathe from the pain.

"You can stop her pain dear Michaelina. All you have to do is be my bride today. Just be My Queen, and all of your Mother's pain will stop. We'll be one big happy family."

"No…No… Michaeli…I mean…Michele. Don't you dare…do anything…he says.

"But if she marries him Claire, you'll be alright. He'll stop torturing you. We did make a promise long ago. Please just let her go through with this. She'll be alright, and then so will you." My mother looks at my father, and speaks with all of the strength and conviction left in her body.

"Anton, you know very well that promise was made long before we knew better. The dissolution to that promise was agreed on by both his clan and ours. I would rather die than have my daughter given away to a monster. Do you hear me, I would rather die."

Even though she was in tremendous pain, she was still fighting for me right up until the end. I can see the life slowly fading from her eyes…for the second time.

"Come now Claire, listen to your wise husband. All you have to do is give her to me and all of this nonsense stops."

With every ounce of strength my mother had

left, she speaks one last time. The silver is eating through her whole body rapidly.

"Go to hell. You will never get her, she will never be yours." She then looks at me.

"Michele, live a happy, full, free life. Just like we have always talked about. I love you my darling daughter."

"I love you too, Mother."

She hangs her head, and lets out one final sigh. My tears start to flow harder, my father puts his head down and sobs softly. I hadn't noticed that Heinrick had nodded again to his personal executioner. But the next thing I see is the huge man with an axe and a long wooden stick, lunge at my mothers' body. With one fell swoop, he drives the stake through her heart and swings the axe against her neck taking her head off.

My father and I scream at the same time.

"NOOOOOOOOOOOO, NOOOOOOOOOO, NOOOOOOOOOO"
I drop to my knees, and cover my face with my hands. The vampires holding me against my will, allow me to fall. They realize in my condition that I will not be able to do anything.

"You murderer! How could you do that? Why…why, did you do it…why??" My father screams at Heinrick hysterically, spittle flying from his mouth. He is inconsolable. Just sobbing and asking why, over and over again under his breath. The tears dripping off of his face.

"Well Anton, I had to make sure there would be no healing, now didn't I?! Plus, it should be a nice incentive for you to give me the answer I want. Since you are a widower now, it's all up to you. Give me Michaelina, and you can live."

I don't think my father heard a word that Heinrick had said. He was going insane with grief, he no longer had any concept of the world around him. He, in a sense is already dead. Dead inside at least, where it really counts.

"ANTON! Get a hold of yourself. We have important matters to rectify. I assumed you would be the one who would be more reasonable. Especially since you have been wavering on your decision to leave the old ways, and wanted to uphold your promise to me."

I am stunned. Through my grief, I hear the words, but don't want to believe them. I look up at my father, he was staring at Heinrick, his face full of vile and hate. He has stopped sobbing now. He looks as if he is weighing every word that he wants to say very carefully before he lets them out of his mouth. Very slowly and succinctly he speaks.

"Yes, I had doubts about our leaving the clan, becoming Newstyles. Yes, heaven help me, I even thought we should honor our original pledge to you, and give you Michaelina as your Queen. But I now know, without any doubts in my mind that my beloved Claire was right all along. Your ways are abominable, and you will never have my child as your bride. I will die today, and take with me the knowledge that she will be free to live her life however she wishes, and any pact made with you hundreds of years ago is no longer valid."

"Is that your final decision, Anton?" My father doesn't answer Heinrick. He stands up as straight as he can, holds his head up high, and looks at me with sadness in his eyes, but so much love on his face.

"I am so sorry Michele. Be happy." He looks at Heinrick intently, then closes his eyes, and he comes to the same end as my mother.

"FATHER, NOOOOOOOO."

I am still on my knees. I have to keep my head down, in my hands. I can no longer look at this room, I will be seeing it in my nightmares forever.

"Well that was rather messy. I really had hoped it wouldn't come to this, but oh well. It is what it is! So, now, Michaelina, since you are an orphan, you are allowed to give your consent to our marriage yourself. Of course, you do realize it's just a technicality now. Since your parents have been disposed of, I will just be taking you anyway. If the clans question it, you will happily say that it was all your decision. That after the awful deaths of your parents at the hand of a robber, you wanted to be taken care of, and you gave yourself to me, and are returning to the old ways. No one will ever be the wiser."

I just stare at him in amazement. Can he really be that sick and twisted?

"NEVER!"

"Oh please don't make this so difficult. I have my ways of making you do whatever I want you to. Surely the events you have just witnessed are solid proof of that."

"You murdering, psychopathic, disease. I will NEVER, EVER, be yours in any way. You will have to kill me too, because I will never leave here with you alive."

"ENOUGH! I am sick of your disagreeable attitude. I see that I have my work cut out for me, all of the brainwashing your parents have done to you. It's just sinful. But I'll get to you and all of that in time. Right now, I have evidence to destroy. Simon, get those things out of here, take them and burn them. Make sure not one ash remains."

I can't believe it, not only has he slaughtered my parents' right in front of my eyes, but now he is going to defile their bodies too…no, no, I'll see him in hell first.

Every bit of anger and hatred that I feel for this creature, comes bubbling to the surface, overflowing, until I can see nothing else but a seething rage. It overtakes me, my body is no longer my own. My emotions are controlling me, no thoughts are involved, only actions.

I spring up off of the floor and jump on the executioner. He still has the bloody axe and stake in his hand. I take him by complete surprise, I'm sure he never expected someone as small as me to attack someone as large as him. But I did! I pounce right on him and take a great big bite out of his neck. I don't need fangs to get a good chunk of flesh ripped from him. He screams in pain, and drops his weapons.

I drop off of him, and grab the tools, just as the two guards who had been restraining me earlier, reach me, I swing the axe with everything I have in me and decapitate both of them.

Simon has been on the ground holding his wounded neck, but when he sees what is happening, he tries getting to his feet. I sense his movement and stake him right to the floor. I then thoroughly enjoy swinging that axe through his beefy neck. Poetic justice I feel.

"*Clap…Clap…Clap…*Well done Michaelina!" I turn around quickly with the axe still in my hand, to see Heinrick standing well out of the way, in a corner, behind the wing chair. He doesn't have any look of fear on his face, the bastard looks happy. I am very disappointed at that.

"I am impressed my dear. It seems I am getting a warrior for a bride. You will be able to fight alongside of me to protect our kingdom. I find your passion for the fight especially exhilarating. You excite me so, and I cannot wait to start our life together."

I am dumbfounded. He still thinks that I am going to be his queen.

"What are you talking about? You don't have a kingdom, you truly are insane."

"I may not have a kingdom yet, but you are the last missing piece to the puzzle. With you at my side, we can have world dominance. Our clan still outnumbers the Newstyles. We can persuade more, and those who won't concede will perish by the sword of my Queen. As for the humans, the ones who serve no viable purpose, and we do not wish to turn, will be used for a food source. We'll just make sure that they keep procreating, so we always have food. Now come, let's get you ready for our departure."

He comes towards me and I raise the axe and swing it in his direction, but he jumps out of the way. I swing it in his new direction and he jumps ahead of me. I take a deep breath and just wait. When I attempt to swing the axe in any direction, he anticipates my moves and gets out of the way in time. How is he doing this?

"I'll be happy to tell you, if you'd like." I am so awestruck, I let the axe slip right out of my hands, and it falls to the floor. He has answered my question but I hadn't said anything out loud.

"It's very simple actually. You were promised to me long before you were even turned. I have studied you, your entire lives, human and vampire. I have been in your mind, I know your every thought and feeling. The ability itself isn't that rare, it just comes with age. You will acquire it too, it just takes hundreds of years and much practice. You will see."

"So you know what I'm thinking all of the time?"

"Most of the time, not all. Some thoughts are easier than others to read. But you are fairly easy, so emotional, your mind speaks very loudly.

He quickly moves behind me, and before I can react, his arm is wrapped tightly around me. It only takes one arm to restrain me. With his free hand, he unzips his pants and lets them fall to his ankles. I do not like what I am feeling pressed up against my ass crack. I start to shake and cry.

"No, no. Get away from me! I don't want you to do this. Please let me go!" My body tightens up as much as it can, as he lifts up my gown and he tries to enter me from behind. I stiffen up and cry out even louder.

"NO! Get off of me, you evil monster!" He whispers in my ear, his acrid breath makes vomit fill my mouth.

"There, there, my Michaelina. You are mine now, and you excite me so. I will have you, I will fuck you whenever I please and you will enjoy it!"

Suddenly, I relax my body. My tears stop falling. This does feel so good, I am really going to like this very much. If only our first time could be more special. Oh, on our wedding night would be so perfect. I have always dreamed of that.

As he bends me over and starts to push himself inside of me, he suddenly stops.

"Oh, yes, yes Michaelina. You are right my beloved. Our first time should be very special. I must try to contain myself, until later tonight. But I will NOT wait any longer than that!" He lets me go, and pulls his pants back up.

"Alright, let's go upstairs. I will allow you to pack a few things to bring with you. Things that you want to have with you for an eternity."

Chapter Twelve

I start moving without even thinking. I can no longer fight my destiny. I will have to learn to accept it, and try to adjust to my new, "old" ways. It's not like I've never heard of the old ways. I had heard all about them from my parents.

My parents' families were devastated when we left their clan, to become "Newstyles." Their clans weren't "Ancients", but they were somewhere in between both sides. Afraid to go against either lifestyle. So I would just be returning to my roots, so to speak. I can do it…and getting the taste for human blood again will be fairly easy. I have to admit, biting that hunk out of Simons flesh felt good, when I have fangs, it'll be even easier. Ohhh, fangs. I've always thought fangs were cool. It'll be so nice to not have them altered anymore. I've always hated that.

Yes, what to pack…well, pictures of my parents of course, gifts they've given me, things to remember them by…yes, looking at poor old Simon right there, I sure did enjoy biting his neck…just felt so damn good…mmmm… *Sluurrpp*… "now die you sick, mother fucker!"

I pull the stake out of Simon, and with all of my force, I heave it right into Heinrick's chest. He is so stunned, he falls backwards against the fireplace. I still have hold of the stake, and I just keep pushing it harder and deeper into his disgusting body, loving every moment of seeing him frightened, and wincing in pain.

"I said die, you sick, filthy, son of a bitch! I hate you and everything that you come from. I'll take you to hell personally before I ever become someone like you."

I love the look of horror in his eyes, and I am taking great pleasure in twisting that stake, and driving it even further in, for everything he has taken from me.

"MICHAELINA STOP!" Startled at the deep, shouting voice, I let go of the stake and turn around to see my Uncle Anthony standing in the doorway. I haven't seen him since our family left the clan, and my mother did not leave things on good terms.

They had said bitter words to each other, and I know that she had regretted some of the things she had said to him the last time she saw him. I often wondered if he had felt that same regret.

"Uncle Anthony…where did you come from? How did you know?"

"Step away from him right now Michaelina. Do you hear me, step away right now!"

"But Uncle, you don't know what he did to my mother and father." I couldn't understand why he was so upset with me. Didn't he understand?

"Yes, I am so sorry my child. We had heard rumors of what Heinrick was planning, and then when we heard that he and his henchmen had gone missing, we surmised what he was up to. I am so sorry that we didn't get here sooner. You poor thing, what you have been through. But it looks like you certainly handled yourself very well! You did all of this carnage by yourself?"

"Yes, I guess I did. After seeing what they did, the horrible torture, the rage just overtook me, and this was the result."

"Always remember that Michaelina. Whenever you need to call on your abilities, they are always there. I would be very pleased if you would practice them even more. But this is not the time to discuss that. Let me clean all of this up for you, go rest now."

Now that I am starting to calm down, the realization of all that has happened, once again hits me, and I start to cry. Uncle Anthony places a cold arm around my shoulder.

"There, there Michaelina. All will be fine. It's just so tragic, it all could've been avoided." I look up at him, at first I assume he means because he hadn't gotten here sooner. But he isn't done speaking.

"My dear stubborn sister. Always such a hard head. All of this nonsense of leaving the clan, and refusing to honor her contract with Heinrick. Just craziness." He is staring at my mothers' decapitated body, shaking his head. I can't believe my ears. I rip myself out of his hold, and look him in the eye, getting as close to his face as I can.

"My mother was so right about you, and *your* family. You disgust me, you are no different than that creature over there. Do me the favor of getting these things out of my home, and then leave, and never return. Just leave me alone to bury my family in private."

"Michaelina, don't be this way, we are family."

"We are no such thing, we are nothing. Now please finish these things off. Heinrick and Simon need to be decapitated, and those other two need to be staked."

"As you wish Michaelina. This is not the

proper time to discuss all of this. The task force is on its' way. We'll get this mess cleaned up, and get out of here immediately. We will talk later."

"My name is Michele, and there is nothing more to discuss, ever. Goodbye." I walk out of the living room, and go upstairs to my bedroom, and never look back.

How come I hadn't remembered that? *I* was the one who maimed Heinrick that horrid night, not the task force as I had thought. I guess I had blocked it all out, too much for me to deal with. Years later when I decided to become a police officer, the task force had gotten word to me that Heinrick had gotten away. He had found the strength to wriggle the stake out of his own body, and had fled so that he could hide and heal. I was never quite sure if that was the truth or not...why didn't Anthony ever tell me that I was the one who had staked Heinrick? If I was able to do it once, surely I can do it again...only this time I'll make sure that he is all the way dead! I'll never leave that to anyone else again!

My head is spinning again, it's getting so dark. I'm in a tunnel, and there's a small ray of light at the end, it's getting closer, and closer still...
I come to in the warehouse, I slowly look around and I am wearing that awful black silk gown, just like the ones that all of the dead women were wearing. The one I wore on that awful night that

149

I had just revisited. I am confused and dazed for a moment, then things get clearer as soon as I hear that deep, rattling voice.

"How nice of you to re-join us Michaelina. I do hope you had nice dreams. As you can see I have taken the opportunity to get you dressed for our nuptials. My child Janella was more than happy to dress you." I look in the direction where Heinrick is nodding, and there is a very tall, redheaded female vampire. Her fangs are fully extended, saliva dripping off of them. She's either hungry or horny, and I don't like the way she is looking at me either way. The thought of her seeing me naked, and touching any part of my body is making me want to vomit. She is every bit as ugly as her maker.

"That will be all for now, Janella. You seem to be making my intended very uncomfortable." Janella gives him a very sour look, and hisses a small, low growl.

"There now, my child. We just need to give Michaelina a little time. She will soon be *very* comfortable with you…as comfortable as I am. So take your leave for now, and we will join up at home shortly, so the celebration can begin. Make sure all of the roses are in full bloom for my Queen's arrival." He then turns to look at me with such a happy, satisfied look on his face. A look that makes my stomach turn even more.

"I have grown a special crop of blue roses for you my lovely bride. Just the perfect shade."

I look up at Ben, his eyes are open and he is looking at me, so sadly. He is having a hard time breathing now. His breaths are shallow and labored and he's pausing in between each one. I immediately fall limp, to my knees, and sob uncontrollably into my hands.

The two large vampires who have been holding me just let me go. They know I am in no condition to do any harm to anyone, or try to escape.

"Oh my poor Michaelina. How it pains me to see you grieve so, for something so common and ordinary. You are destined for greatness, and once you are by my side, I will give you the world." I very slowly take my hands from my face, and look up at his face.

"I give up Heinrick. I can no longer fight my destiny. You win. I will be your bride." I can hardly speak the words, but I continue.

"I will do whatever you want, I am all yours. Can we please just get out of here? I can't look at…him…anymore." The words stick in my throat and burn like acid.

Heinrick looks absolutely thrilled and delighted.

"Oh I just knew you would come to your senses someday. You have pleased me so. Yes,

yes, of course we can leave this awful place. Come let us go to our nest. Where we will be wed, and start our life together blissfully after satisfying our lustful hungers tonight." He floats over to me, and reaches out his hand to me. I hesitantly place my hand in his, and squeeze tightly. The look of shear happiness on his face is practically making him glow.

"Mi...ch...ele... nooo, pleeaassee...don't..."

I can't look at Ben. His voice is barely more than a whisper. I close my eyes, take a deep breath, and start rising to my feet. I grab Heinrick's other hand since I stumble slightly as I get up. He is trying to steady me, and with one swift move, I swing him around with all my might and throw him into his two henchmen. Racing to a stack of boxes in front of me, I leap up on them. Within a second I am on the plank near Ben. The huge vampire standing between me and Ben has no time to react, and I pull the saw right out of his hand and slash his throat with it. I bring the saw back the other way, and his body falls off of the plank to the concrete floor below, and his head goes rolling in the opposite direction.

"You stupid, foolish girl! You may have escaped me once, but you never will again." Heinrick is screaming up to me. He turns to his goons and screeches at them.

"You idiots, why are you just standing there? Seize her!"

I look at Ben and wink, he looks amazed, and is trying to smile at me. Out of the corner of my eye, I see the two guards flying for me. I tear off a piece of the wooden railing from the plank, and with every ounce of strength I have, I force it into the first vampires' heart and it goes all the way through to the second vampire.

I am even a little amazed at that one. But now for the best part, getting my hands on Heinrick. I see him, he is still right where I left him standing, in complete shock. Our eyes lock, and he knows I am coming for him.

"How could you do this to me Michaelina? I love you, and always have. You are my destiny, you agreed to be my Queen, you promised to be mine."

"You stupid, vile, creature. How could you ever believe for one second that I would ever, ever, even consider marrying you? You don't know what love is, it's sacrilegious for you to even use that word. You disgust me. I find you revolting and I loathe you and your kind. I would rather be dead, permanently, than to be anywhere near you, ever. This will be the happiest day of my life, the day that I destroy you forever."

I slowly start to come down onto the same

stack of boxes, Heinrick seems transfixed, as if he still thinks he can win me over. He has a look of determination on his face, or maybe it's just insanity.

"If you kill me, you lose everything. Your kingdom, and all of the riches I will lay at your feet."

"I don't want your kingdom, I don't want anything from you. You tortured and slaughtered my parents' right in front of my eyes. You have killed more innocent women than can be counted, and you are killing the only man I'll ever love. The only thing left for me is to make sure you die a very painful death, so I can send you straight to hell where you belong." The look on his face is no longer determined, it's all insanity now.

"Well, if I can't have you, then no one else ever will either." Heinrick starts to move, coming towards me. I step back a little on the stack and I see something shiny sticking out from under one of the boxes that I didn't see when I ran up on here the first time. It's an axe!

I plunge to grab it, just as Heinrick should have reached me, but he isn't near me. I look and see him leaping on a different set of boxes, and he's heading up…oh no…no…it's extremely clear now exactly where he's headed.

"LEAVE HIM ALONE!!!" I jump back up

on the plank, and race towards Ben, hoping to get to him before Heinrick does. We reach him at the same time, and without any thought in my head other than stopping Heinrick from inflicting any more pain on my beloved Ben, I lift the axe over my head and heave it directly at Heinrick's chest.

The axe hits him directly in the heart, before he has any time to react.

"Nooooooo…ahhhhhhhhhhhhhhhh." The force of the axe hitting him, knocks him right off of the plank, and he falls to the floor below. He hits the concrete with a thud. I look down at him, and with the axe sticking out of his chest, he is lying motionless with his eyes closed.

I rush to Ben, he can barely keep his eyes even slightly open. His breathing is even more labored. Up close, I can see how badly he's really hurt. His body is nothing but bruises and blood, his eye lids are so swollen, and he cannot open his eyes wider than two slits. His skin is burned deeply where the chains are touching it. In some spots his bones are visible.

With a trembling hand, I stroke his glorious face. He opens his eyes as wide as he is able to.

"Hel…lo…se…xy…" It's taking all of his strength just to say those two words.

"Shhh, my love. Save your energy. I am going to find something to cut these chains with and get you down from here. Just please hang on for me Ben, just hang on for me." He moves his head slowly from side to side.

"No…it's…too…late…for…me. I'm…not…go…ing…to…make…it." Tears flood my cheeks, but I try to keep my composure for him.

"No Ben, don't you dare say that. You are going to make it! I am getting you out of here, and you are going to live a long, happy life. With me, if you'll have me after everything that has happened here tonight."

"So…per…fect. Just…know…one thi…ng. That I…love…you. Al…ways." He is so exhausted from speaking, his head drops down on his bare, bloodied chest.

I close my eyes and hang my head too. I can't bear to see him die. *No, noooo, not him. Oh, please don't take him from me…please.*

"Bravo Michaelina, Bravo." I open my eyes and look to my right to see Uncle Anthony standing there.

"I am very impressed, and I have to admit more than a little proud too. I knew you could do it, if you would just embrace your heritage."

"How nice of you to finally show up Uncle. I could've used your help earlier."

"We are here now to clean up. We'll get your friend down from there, and you can take him home." Tears flow more steadily now.

"I think it's too late for him…he's barely breathing. I don't think he's going to make it."

"Nonsense. Don't be silly. He's in bad shape, but he'll be fine. Here give him this."

He throws something to me, and I catch it in midair. It's a syringe. I look at my uncle quizzically.

"What is this?"

"Just something to help the healing process. He's pretty bad, this will assist the normal healing. He'll still need to recuperate, but he'll be fine in a week or two. Of course he'll start healing as soon as we get those chains off of him."

He snaps his fingers and my cousins, Jonathan and Matthias, walk towards us with special heavy duty gloves on. Of course, the silver chains….the SILVER chains…

It slowly starts making sense to me, and I quickly jab the needle into Bens' arm and press all of the clear liquid into him. For the first time during this whole nightmare, I have a glimmer of hope that he'll be alright.

My cousins cut the chains, and slowly pull them from Ben's skin, some of the charred skin is lifting off with the silver. It is agony seeing him like this, thankfully he's passed out. His body has withstood all of the pain that it can.

They lift him down gently, and we all drop down to the floor below us. I kneel on the floor, and cradle Ben's head in my lap, as I stroke his hair and face. His color is getting better already and his bruises are getting lighter. His eyes slowly open, and he looks up at my face.

"Ben, I am so happy to see you." The tears flow again, but they are tears of happiness this time.

He can speak with slightly more strength now.

"Michele, my love. Thank you."

"For what?"

"For saving my life. For loving me so much, that you were willing to give your life for mine. But I would never have wanted you to do that. I'd rather be dead than be without you."

"Don't you see…I have no life without you either."

"You were so amazing tonight, by the way. I didn't know…"

"Well I didn't know about you either. I guess the blitztreach overpowered us completely! Whoever would've thought that two vampires would meet during a police ride along and find their life mates in each other." We simply smile.

"My mom always told me, one day this would happen to me. But I thought it was just something out of one of her romance novels. I am so glad she was right and I was wrong."

"I am equally as thrilled that it's real. I love you Ben. Forever."

"I love you too Michele, and you'd better believe its forever." I carefully lift his head up as I bend mine down, and we kiss. I honestly didn't think I would ever feel those tender lips on mine again, I shuddered at the thought.

"Mmm, even sweeter than I remember. Help me sit up please, love?"

"Are you sure? Are you strong enough?"

"Yeah, I can feel the healing progressing very rapidly. I am actually feeling pretty good. But I think being in your arms has something to do with that." I roll my eyes and chuckle. It feels so good to laugh. I wasn't sure if I would ever be doing that again.

"Okay, are you ready? I am going to slide you against the box right behind us."

"Yep, let's do it." I slowly lift him up and slide him gently, just a foot or so, and lean him against the large box. Once I have him steadied against it, he takes my hands in his, and he looks deep into my eyes.

"I know that we are not in the best surroundings right now, and this may not be the perfect time, but all I know is that we are both here, together, alive." We both smile at that word…since technically we really aren't. But I guarantee no two people feel more alive than we do right at this very moment.

"I love you more than I have ever loved anyone in my entire life. I love you with all of my heart and with everything that I am. Michele Murphy, will you please make me the happiest man on earth, and do me the honor of marrying me?"

Just at that very moment, light and sunshine fill the room. I am overflowing with happiness, and have never been more full of love.

"I too love you more than I have ever loved anyone. I love you with my whole heart, and all that I am. Nothing would make me happier than spending eternity with you. Yes, Ben, Yes I will be proud and honored to be your wife." We kiss oh so softly.

"Excuse me Michaelina. But we are almost done with the cleanup, I think it would be for the best if the two of you leave now."

When Uncle Anthony speaks it sounds more like an order than a suggestion. It hits me that I still have some unfinished business to take care of before I leave here and begin my new, wonderful life. I kiss Ben, and start to stand up.

"Excuse me a minute, my love. There's something I need to take care of before we go home. I'll be right back."

"Go right ahead. I'll be right here waiting for

you." There's that sweet smile that I will never get tired of seeing!

I walk over to my uncle and stand right in front of him.

"Yes, Michaelina. What can I do for you?"

"You can answer something for me. Did you allow Heinrick to escape each time?"

"You don't understand Michaelina. We had many things to learn from him. It's not as simple as doing away with someone because they are *bad*. There is a reason for good and bad in this world. You are either too young to understand that yet or too stubborn. You have a human perspective, which I don't blame you for entirely. It's the way you were raised." I am heartsick and appalled.

"After seeing what that *thing* did to your own sister, how could you let him live? It is not being immature or stubborn to know that something that crazed and heartless would not only kill again, but he would eventually come after me?"

"Of course I knew he'd return and kill again. Human life doesn't mean to me what it means to you and your kind. Humans are expendable. Yes, I also strongly suspected that he would come for you, but I knew you'd be able to take care of yourself when the time came. I was right too. Look around this room. You had no help, this was all you, being vampire. Tell me, didn't that feel wonderful? The abilities coming out like that, the power, the kill?"

I am in amazement, nothing makes this man bend at all.

"You want to know what felt great? Saving the man I love and myself from that madman. Killing the creature that murdered my parents and so many innocents. In fact, I don't think I quite finished that yet, did I?"

I walk over to where Heinrick's body is, with the axe still sticking out of his chest. As I stand over him, he opens his eyes, he's in bad shape, but not bad enough. He would eventually heal from this wound too. I'll never let that happen again. It's happened too many times, too many lives have been lost.

"Oh my lovely Michaelina, I knew you'd come back for me and save me."

"Think again you sick fuck!" I pull the axe from his chest, hard, so he can feel it. He yells out in pain.

"NO, Michaelina! Stop, let me handle this. I'll take care of it."

"Never again Uncle…Never!" Heinrick is looking at me with such pleading in his eyes, I spit on his face.

"Go to hell." With all of the strength in my body, I put the axe right through his neck. Now that feels wonderful!

Ben is smiling widely at me, my uncle just starts shaking his head.

"Oh my poor misguided Michaelina. I was so hoping that someday you'd embrace the vampire ways, and come back into the clan."

"That's what is so funny, Uncle. I do embrace the vampire ways. The vampire ways of my parents. I am proud to be vampire. Maybe a little more so tonight...but I will never come back to your clan. Vampires no longer need to be dark, sinister, killers. Like the creatures in the old human legends. We love being in the human world, taking some of their traits. We are happy just as we are."

"It's all such nonsense Michaelina. Someday, maybe you'll come to your senses. I hope for that still." I shake my head in disbelief, he hasn't heard a word I've said.

"You will never understand. So I am telling you for the last time. My name is Michele, and there is nothing more to say...ever. Goodbye."

I go straight back to where Ben is sitting. Uncle Anthony has turned and glided away quietly. Ben has a look of concern. I sit down next to him, and kiss his cheek.

"Are you okay Michele?"

"Yes, I really am. I am feeling pretty damn good right now. How are you feeling sweetheart? Are you strong enough to stand, so we can go home?"

"I think I just need another minute or two, and I'll be able to walk. Did you mean what you said about being happy to be vampire, and embracing some vampire ways?"

"Yes I did. Does that bother you?"

"No not at all. On the contrary, I am thrilled about that. My mom and dad raised me to be very proud of our heritage. Even though we can't fully disclose ourselves as such, and we inherit so many human traits, it's still nice to honor being vampire. To let our fangs down…so to speak." We share a soft laugh.

"I agree completely, my love. You know, we are starting our own clan now. We can adopt our own ways, and find what feels best for us."

"Hmmm, speaking of that…how do you feel about letting our fangs grow in? I cannot tell you how much I have wanted to bite you since the moment I met you!" I throw my head back and laugh. More from relief than anything.

"I have been wanting to do the same to you…so that's a great big YES! Oh, I love you Ben."

"I love you too Michele. Let's go home!"

I help him to his feet, we hold onto each other tightly, and walk out of that warehouse. Leaving all of the past horrors behind, and heading towards a future full of sunshine!

Chapter Thirteen

Six weeks later…

I am looking at my reflection in the full length mirror in the Wildwood motel room. I never envisioned this day happening in my life. I have never been so happy.

"Oh my dear, you look positively radiant! You are going to take Bens' breath away."

"Thank you Brenda. I have to admit, I do feel radiant today."

"It's such a perfect day for a wedding too. The sun is shining so brightly, a slight ocean breeze, it's just right."

"Knock, knock, can I come in ladies?"

"Yes dear, come in."

"Michele, you look beautiful. I knew you'd be

a stunning bride, and I was right."

"Thank you Gary. I hope your son agrees with you!"

"Of course he will, he has my superior taste in women!" Brenda and Gary hug and kiss. They are so loving and so adorable together. So much in love, they act as if they are still on their honeymoon even after all the years they have been together. I have a feeling that's exactly how Ben and I will always be too.

"Thank you both for welcoming me into your family as you have. I have come to love the two of you as much as Ben does." Brenda hugs me tightly.

"My dear, we love you like a daughter. We couldn't have picked a better mate for our son. You make him happier than we have ever seen him. Thank you for that."

"Oh believe me, it is purely my pleasure. He is my happiness!"

"Well, all of the guests are here now, so are you ladies ready?"

"Just one minute Gary. I want to give something to Michele." Brenda takes a small red velvet box from her purse and places it in my hand.

"I know that you are missing your parents today, but if they were here they would tell you how very proud they are of you, and how much they love you. I also know as a mother, that your mother would've wanted you to have something special on your wedding day. This belonged to my mother. I wore it on my wedding day, and now it's your turn my lovely daughter."

I open the box, and see the most beautiful necklace. A small delicate diamond heart, with a heart shaped emerald in the very center.

"Oh, it is gorgeous. I will proudly wear it, always. I love it. Thank you so much!" The three of us hug and kiss. Happy tears in Brenda's and my eyes.

"Okay, you two, no tears. It'll mess up your make up, and then we'll never get this thing started." Brenda and I both laugh, we know he's right.

"Okay, okay. We'll leave you alone now Michele so you can finish getting ready. Oh, and Gary and I have discussed this. We know that we will never take the place of your own parents, but if you ever choose to call us Mom and Dad, we would be honored."

"I think I would really like that. Thank you for everything, Mom and Dad. I love you both very much." We smile warmly at each other, and they leave to take their seats.

I take one last look in the mirror, fluff my loosely hanging hair, adding a few tiny, sparkly flowers here and there. It's just the way Ben likes it. I smooth out my dress, making sure it's hanging just right on me. The chiffon flows so softly, and oh so delicately. It is the slightest shade of blush, with thin, jeweled straps. A beaded empire waist, ruched bust, and it falls softly down into a chapel length train. I place Brenda's gift around my neck. I reapply one last touch of lip gloss, and I do believe I am all ready to see my groom. I grab my bouquet of miniature pale pink roses, and head for the beach.

There is Jack, waiting for me at the beginning of the sandy aisle. He smiles at me, and takes my arm, and we wait for the music to begin. So much love in the air today. Friends and family. All of Ben's relatives of course, but now they would be mine too. They are all here to share in our happiness.

I look up into Jack's face. He is smiling brightly at me. He looks as proud as my own father would be.

As Debussy's "Claire de Lune" starts to play, we walk down the beach and there he is, my Ben. So ruggedly and incredibly handsome in his beige dress shirt and linen pants, the sun shining on his thick sandy hair. He is beaming from ear to ear. He apparently likes what he sees too.

The sand feels delightful in between my toes, I am barefoot of course. As we reach Ben at the ocean's edge, Jack places my hand in Bens'. He gives me a sweet kiss on the cheek, and then goes and sits next to Betty.

The minister smiles at us, and she begins speaking. Ben and I face each other, beaming, and holding hands.

"Welcome to the joining of two hearts, and two lives. We are all here today to celebrate Ben and Michele's happiness, and share in their love. Love is a rare gift, something to be treasured, to be shared. The endless love that a husband and wife share is even more precious. A true gift that they give to one another every day, forever. As Ben and Michele pledge their lives, love, and hearts to each other today, let's rejoice in their happiness, and their gift of love." She turns to Ben.

"Ben, do you accept Michele as your life mate? Do you promise to love, honor, cherish, and respect her eternally?"

"Oh, Yes I do! I very much do!" The guests giggle at Ben's enthusiasm. We haven't stopped smiling at each other yet. Now the minister turns to me.

"Michele, do you accept Ben as your life mate? Do you promise to love, honor, cherish and respect him eternally?"

"Yes, I very much do too!"

"Please place these rings on each other's

fingers to symbolize the eternal circle of love, honor, trust, and respect that you are pledging to each other today." We place our beautiful platinum bands on each other.

"I happily announce that you are husband and wife. Ben you may kiss your bride!"

The guests rise and applaud, as Ben and I embrace each other and kiss. Such a perfect ceremony, a perfect day…

As the sun sets on the waves, we are still celebrating on the beach. Everyone is dancing and eating and laughing, and just enjoying the happiness of the day.
Ben and I are beyond ecstatic, and can't stop holding and kissing each other.

"In case I forgot to tell you earlier, you are absolutely breathtaking, my sexy bride."

"You are looking pretty stunning yourself."

"I love you Mrs. Brewer."

"Oh, say it again, and again…"

"I love you Mrs. Michele Brewer. Oh, I do love saying that. *Mrs. Brewer*, I love you!"

"I will never get tired of hearing it either. I love you so much Ben, my wonderful husband!"

"What a very lucky husband I am too. So, my lovely wife, can we please, please, leave for our honeymoon now?"

"Oh hell yes…let's go. Let's get started on the beginning of our eternity together."

As the orchestra plays, Ben spins me around one last time, and pulls me close to him.

We kiss, and smile at each other, as the moonlight shines on our fangs...

"The Beginning"

I would like to thank all of my friends, you know who you are! Thank you for being the amazing people that you are! Each and every one of you are my rocks! You are always there with love, support and compassion. Oh, and lots of laughs too! I love all of you so very much! Thank you for being in my life.

Thank you, K! Just for being so completely awesome, for just being you! Thank you so much for all of your help!! I never could've hit the "publish" button without you!! Love you, K!

Thank you Janette Dionne for "Heinrick".

Thank you to my two older brothers, Tom and Bob. Just for being my big brothers, in every sense of those words. Love you both!

Love you, Dinky! You are my sweet little girl, and you make me smile every day!

I would not be the woman that I am today without your love and guidance, Momma. I hope you are proud! I love and miss you, always.

Music has always been such a huge part of my life. I thank my Mom for that. I can never remember one day in my life where there wasn't some type of music playing. On the radio, or Mom playing her 45's. I feel like my life has had its very own soundtrack. Music has been a part of every good time and every sad time.

Growing up, there were the piano lessons, vocal lessons, all of the family parties on every occasion. The sleepovers, Christmases, Easters, Halloweens and all of the many trips to Wildwood every summer. All with their own songs that fill my memories.

I have loved everything from country to rock to classical to pop. I still have music in the background of my life each and every day. So, of course, the writing of this book has also had its own soundtrack. During the course of the writing, rewriting, editing, rewriting again, formatting, and of course, more editing.

I have mainly listened to two incredible artists, who inspire me, make me smile, make me happy…just make me *feel*. So, from the bottom of my heart, a huge Thank You to Kenny Chesney and Maroon 5! Your CD's have been with me every step of the way! You've gotten me through some very tough times, and have helped me celebrate the great times with this book! Please keep the music going, I have quite a few more books left in me to write!

Darlene Chavis